Man of the Moment

Born in London in 1939, Alan Ayckbourn spent
most of his childhood in Sussex and was educated
at Haileybury. Leaving there one Friday at the age
of seventeen, he went into the theatre the following
Monday and has been working in it ever since as,
variously, a stage manager, sound technician,
lighting technician, scene painter, prop-maker,
actor, writer and director. These talents developed
thanks to his mentor, Stephen Joseph, whom he
first met in 1958 upon joining the newly formed
Library Theatre in Scarborough. He was a BBC
Radio Drama Producer from 1965 to 1970,
returning to Scarborough to take up the post of
Artistic Director of the Theatre in the Round, left
vacant after Stephen Joseph's death in 1967. Since
that time, he has premièred over thirty of his plays,
first at the Library Theatre and, from 1976
onwards, at the company's new converted base, the
Stephen Joseph Theatre. Over twenty of his plays
have subsequently been produced either in the
West End or at the National Theatre. They have
been translated into twenty-four languages and
have been performed in virtually every continent of
the globe, receiving many national and
international awards in the process.

MAN OF
THE MOMENT

ALAN AYCKBOURN

faber and faber
LONDON · BOSTON

First published in 1990
by Faber and Faber Limited
3 Queen Square London WC1N 3AU
Reprinted 1990

Photoset by Parker Typesetting Service Leicester
Printed in England by Clays Ltd, St Ives plc

A CIP record for this book is available from the British
Library

ISBN 0-571-15475-1

CHARACTERS

VIC PARKS
TRUDY, his wife
CINDY, aged seven, their daughter
SHARON GIFFIN, their children's nanny
RUY, their Spanish gardener
MARTA, Ruy's wife, their Spanish maid
KENNY COLLINS, Vic's manager
JILL RILLINGTON
DOUGLAS BEECHEY
ASHLEY BARNES, a TV floor manager
plus
seven ACTORS (six non-speaking)

Setting: The patio/pool area of Vic and Trudy's
Mediterranean villa.

Time: One day, recently.

Man of the Moment was first performed in Scarborough at the Stephen Joseph Theatre in the Round on 10 August 1988. The cast was as follows:

JILL RILLINGTON	Lynette Edwards
TRUDY	Lesley Meade
KENNY COLLINS	Simon Chandler
RUY	Daniel Collings
DOUGLAS BEECHEY	Jon Strickland
VIC PARKS	Peter Laird
CINDY	Lisa Bailey *or* Charlotte Kershaw
SHARON GIFFIN	Shirley-Anne Selby
MARTA	Doreen Andrew
ASHLEY BARNES	Peter Forbes
DAVID	Adam Godley

Directed by Alan Ayckbourn
Designed by Michael Holt

It was subsequently performed at the Globe Theatre, London, on 14 February 1990. The cast was as follows:

JILL RILLINGTON	Samantha Bond
TRUDY	Diane Bull
KENNY COLLINS	Simon Chandler
RUY	Daniel Collings
DOUGLAS BEECHEY	Michael Gambon
VIC PARKS	Peter Bowles
CINDY	Joanna Relf *or* Diana Endsor
SHARON GIFFIN	Shirley-Anne Selby
MARTA	Doreen Andrew
ASHLEY BARNES	Terence Booth
DAVID	Paul Stewart

Directed by Alan Ayckbourn
Designed by Roger Glossop

ACT I

The paved patio/pool area of a modern, moderate-sized (three-bedroomed) villa in a Spanish-speaking area of the Mediterranean. At one side, a glimpse of the villa itself. White stucco walls and wooden shutters. The edge of the living area – tiled floor with rugs – perhaps the end of what promises to be a very long drinks bar. Large, open sliding doors leading out from the living area on to a shaded area. Here, a table and chairs to seat about four. Moving away from the house further, a step down to a slightly sunken sun-bathing area. Here, two or three sun loungers and a low table. At the other side, steps up again to the back gate of the villa, which in turn leads to a carport and the rough road.

Also visible, the raised, angled corner of the swimming pool (deep end). It is possible to walk around the pool, either along the deep end to reach the diving board (unseen) or along the poolside to reach the shallow end.

One or two shrubs in tubs. Perhaps a toy left lying about, betraying the presence of young children.

At the start, though, none of this is visible. Just a light on JILL RILLINGTON *who sits on the patio in a chair beside the table, angled out facing away from the house.* JILL *is in her early thirties and looking good – certainly at first glance. Every inch the assured, charming TV reporter/presenter.*

She is at present doing a piece to camera, though we won't guess this immediately. The film crew are out of sight and remain so throughout. Sometimes we will hear their distant voices calling to JILL *but their words are impossible to decipher.*

JILL: *(To camera)* Hallo. I'm Jill Rillington. In this edition of *Their Paths Crossed*, we tell a story that started seventeen years ago in the slow and sneet of a Surrey Novem . . . Oh, piss! Keep rolling. We'll go again. Snow and sleet. Snow and sleet . . . *(Slowly.)* Snow – and – sleet . . . Here we go. Snow and sleet. Hallo. I'm Rill Jillington . . . My God, I don't believe this – Right, straight in – keep turning. Hallo. I'm Jill Rillington. In this edition of *Their Paths Crossed*, we tell a story that started seventeen years ago in the snow and sleet of a Surrey November morning and finishes – (*She gestures. As she does so, the lights spread out to include the whole area, rather as if the camera had pulled back to include her surroundings. We see she is wearing a discreet radio mic attached to her blouse. On the table beside her is a cardboard folder containing research material, press clippings and interview notes.*) – here. In the brilliant sunshine of a glorious Mediterranean summer. It's a story which has – fittingly perhaps – almost a fairy-tale ring to it. A tale with a hero and a villain – even a damsel in distress. But this is no child's fable, it is a true story. This is the real world where nothing is as it seems. This is the real world where heroes are easily forgotten; this is the real world where the villains may, themselves, become heroes. And as for distressed damsels – well, are they in reality ever truly rescued? I'll leave you, the viewer, to judge for yourself . . . (*She pauses for a moment, looking towards the camera.*) And – cut! OK?

(*A shout of assent from the crew.*)

Did you get the wide? (*Gesturing.*) The wide?

(*Crew replies.*)

Good. Did you get this whole area? (*Gesturing and yelling.*) This whole area?

(*A yell from one of the crew.*)

What? (*She notices her radio mic.*) Oh, yes. Sorry, Dan. Didn't mean to burst your eardrums. Sorry, my love. (*She consults her watch. She makes to yell again then thinks better of it.*) George – (*Quietly.*) Sorry, love. Dan, can you tell George to set up the arrival shot. For the arrival. Can he do that? Where we talked about? On the bend? So we see this man's taxi coming up the hill and their first meeting at the front door? OK? George knows where. I'll be with you in a sec. Thank you, love. I'll unplug. Save your batteries.

(*She unplugs her mic from its transmitter in her pocket and tucks away the lead. As she is doing this,* TRUDY *comes out from the house rather tentatively. She is only a few years older than* JILL *but looks rather more. Possibly due to an over-eagerness to please her husband* VIC, TRUDY *has attempted to retain the look of*

2

someone ten years younger; an image presumably with which he originally fell in love. She has taken rather more care than usual this morning as the TV cameras are about.)

TRUDY: Sorry. Is it all right for me –?

JILL: Yes, we've finished. It's quite all right.

TRUDY: Would you all care for coffee? A cup of coffee?

JILL: Well, I'd love one. I think the crew are probably OK. They seem to have brought their own – refreshments.

TRUDY: Sure?

JILL: No, it's probably best to let them get on. We need to set up for this new shot. I want to catch Mr Beechey actually arriving here straight from his hotel . . .

TRUDY: Yes, yes, yes . . .

JILL: And hopefully his first meeting with your husband . . .

TRUDY: Yes, yes. I don't know if Vic's . . .

JILL: Is he still not back?

TRUDY: Well, he should be. He said he would be. (*Moving to the gate.*) Kenny was going to see if he could . . . Just a minute, I'll . . . (*Calling to someone.*) Kenny, is he coming? Can you see them? No?

JILL: No?

TRUDY: No, I'm sorry. He only took the children down to the beach. With Sharon. She's their nanny. You can usually see them on the beach down there . . . He did promise he'd be here . . .

JILL: (*Rather coolly*) Yes, he did.

TRUDY: It's not like him to do this. I'll make the coffee. It may have just slipped his mind. (*Smiling.*) Once he gets with the kids . . .

(TRUDY *hurries back into the house.*)

JILL: (*Smiling*) Yes. (*Sourly, looking at her watch again.*) Bugger him.

(*She is gathering up her folder from the table as* KENNY *comes through the back gate. Late twenties or early thirties. He is one of the new breed of young manager/agents with a cool, laid-back, slightly public school, unflappable exterior which just serves to conceal any insecurity beneath.*)

KENNY: No. No sign.

JILL: Well, where is he?

KENNY: Digging on the beach. Burying the kids. Bonking the nanny. I don't know.

JILL: But he knew about this. He knew . . .

KENNY: Oh, yes, he knew all right.

JILL: I mean you knew it, Kenny, we talked about it last night . . .

KENNY: I know, he definitely knew . . .

JILL: He knew I wanted to catch their first meeting . . .

KENNY: I know, I know . . .

JILL: I needed that on camera. He knew that.

KENNY: I know, he knew. He said you'd said it to him, I know . . .

JILL: I said it to him. You know I did.

KENNY: I know. He knew, all right, he knew . . .

JILL: Then why the hell isn't he here if he knew?

KENNY: I don't know. (*Pause.*) You know Vic.

JILL: Yes.

KENNY: You can't tell him.

JILL: I don't see what makes him so special.

KENNY: He's a star, darling. A star. Isn't he? (*Pause.*) He won't let you down. Don't worry.

JILL: There's no point in saying that. He just has.

KENNY: You can film it later. The meeting. You can mock it up later.

JILL: I doubt it.

KENNY: Why not? Vic can do that. He's a pro. He's used to that. He did a programme once. Visiting sick kids in hospital. He was 140 miles away in a London studio. No one ever knew. Except the kids he was meant to be visiting. He can do that sort of thing. Piece of cake.

JILL: I'm sure Vic could. I'm not so sure about Mr Beechey.

KENNY: No?

JILL: No.

KENNY: Not your television natural, I take it?

JILL: He's about as lively as a sheet of laminated chipboard. I've just spent four days interviewing Mr Beechey. In his home town of Purley. I think I've got about twenty seconds of

4

usable material. And those are the shots of Purley.

KENNY: Not a talker?

JILL: Oh, he talks. It's just he never says anything. You know, when I first started out with the BBC as a radio interviewer, I went on this course and they warned us that one day we'd all of us find ourselves interviewing the uninterviewable. I thought, after ten years, I'd managed to escape. And then along comes Mr Beechey. (*Musing.*) It's not that he won't talk. You can usually cope with that. We all get that. Then you can generally coax them round. Eventually. Or you say something so blatantly incorrect about them, they're forced to contradict you in self-defence. But this man, he's deadly. The point is, there's absolutely nothing you can say to him that he doesn't agree with. He smothers you with approval. It's like interviewing a fire blanket.

KENNY: You normally only meet people like that during general elections, don't you? What about Mrs Beechey? Any joy with her?

JILL: She spent the four days we were there hiding in the boxroom. I never got to speak to her at all. All I'm hoping is, once he's here – far away from the bright lights of Purley – he might open up.

KENNY: (*Wandering to the gate to look*) A little sunshine. Does wonders.

JILL: Is Vic coming?

KENNY: Can't see him.

JILL: Listen, Kenny, I hope he's taking this seriously . . .

KENNY: Of course. You know Vic. He's a pro . . .

JILL: I mean, this may just be another tacky little interview as far as he's concerned . . .

KENNY: He's never said that –

JILL: . . . a jokey programme which only merits an eighth of his attention . . .

KENNY: Whoever said that – ?

JILL: . . . but for me this is important. It may not seem much to you, but if this works out – then I have their firm provisional promise of the other seven slots. That is eight in all . . .

KENNY: (*Duly impressed*) Eight, heavens!

JILL: Plus – plus – wait for it! Plus another pencilled second series of eight in the New Year.

KENNY: Sixteen, goodness . . .

JILL: Right. Sixteen. Of my own series. Seventy per cent film – thirty per cent studio – me – nobody else – me alone –

KENNY: (*Humouring her along*) That's some doing. These days.

JILL: Oh, I know a lot of people are sitting back there waiting for me to fall flat on my arse. Colin and Martin thing. Clare. She certainly is. And that Richard – whatsit. They are all dying for that to happen . . . Well, I've got this far and no one is going to trip me up now. I've fought for this chance – just watch me go . . .

KENNY: I will. I will . . .

JILL: Not Mr Beechey, not you, not Vic, not that damp, septic tank of a film crew I've been landed with – and I know who saddled me with them, thank you very much, Mrs McIver, I'll settle you when I get back home, madam, see if I don't – God, is this mic still on? No . . . Oh, relief . . . Kenny, if the choice is this or making ten-minute promo videos of eager fringe companies from Stockport for the British Council, I know which I want to do. Just remember Vic owes me, Kenny. He owes me one. I helped him. Remember that. (*Pointing to herself.*) This kid from BBC Radio Bristol got that whole splendid career of his started. Remember that.

KENNY: All right, all right.

JILL: Just remember.

KENNY: All right. Easy.

(*Pause.* JILL *simmers.*)

We love you. Promise. We're all mad about you.

JILL: (*Muttering*) I don't want love, I just want basic co-operation, all right?

KENNY: (*Moving back to the gate*) Relax.

JILL: (*Looking at her watch again*) He should be here. Why isn't he here? Neither of them are here. This is all I need.

KENNY: It's only one minute past.

JILL: By the time they get here, that film crew will want a break. I've never met anything like them. Every time they change film they have a union meeting. And it's no use trying to do anything after lunch, because they're all totally legless. There's that much camera shake, you'd think we were filming on the top of Mount Etna . . .

KENNY: (*Still at the gate*) There's a car in the distance just starting up the hill.

JILL: Is it Vic?

KENNY: No, it's not the jeep. It looks like a taxi from here. Probably your Mr Beechey.

JILL: Right. Well, we can film him arriving, anyway. Get his reactions. If he has any. Keep a look out for Vic. (*As she goes.*) You're his agent, get him here.

KENNY: His manager . . .

(JILL *hurries out through the garden gate.*)

JILL: (*Calling*) George! Come on, get a move on. He's coming! Come on, come on!

(*As* JILL *goes,* TRUDY *comes out from the house with a tray of coffee things.*)

TRUDY: Is something happening?

KENNY: I think Mr Beechey's arrived.

TRUDY: (*Without enthusiasm*) Oh. Good.

KENNY: What's the matter? Nervous?

TRUDY: Not at all.

KENNY: It was years ago. You weren't even around.

TRUDY: You know perfectly well how I feel about all this.

KENNY: All right.

TRUDY: I blame you. You talked him into it. This programme.

KENNY: When have I ever talked Vic into anything? When has anyone? Come on. Don't blame me. Be honest. Have *you*? Have you ever talked him into anything?

(TRUDY *doesn't reply.*)

(*His point proved*) Well, then.

TRUDY: He said he'd be back by now. He's forgotten. I bet that's what's happened. He always forgets what he doesn't choose to remember.

KENNY: Sharon might have reminded him.

TRUDY: (*With ill-concealed dislike*) Well, I think telling the time's a bit beyond Sharon. I'd better fetch another cup. (*She makes to leave.*)

7

KENNY: Haven't you got anyone to help you today?

TRUDY: How do you mean?

KENNY: You know. To make the coffee? Fetch things out?

TRUDY: Oh, yes. Marta's here. Only by the time I've explained it to her, it's quicker to do it myself. I mean, she can speak quite good English. I know she can. She always understands Vic. It's just me. She doesn't seem to understand me at all. It's probably the way I talk, I don't know . . .

(TRUDY *goes back into the house.* KENNY *wanders to the pool. He stoops and tests the water temperature with his hand. As he is doing this,* RUY, *a man in his fifties, comes through the back gate with a pool rake. He ignores* KENNY, *as he ignores everyone, except on those rare occasions when* VIC *speaks to him.*)

KENNY: Good morning to you.

(RUY *totally ignores him. He starts to rake the surface of the pool. This activity soon takes him out of view.*)

(*Sarcastically, in response to* RUY's *lack of response*) Thank you. And the same to you. Lovely chatting to you. Now, you must excuse me interrupting but I have to get on. Not at all. And the same to you.

(TRUDY *enters from the house.*)

TRUDY: (*Talking to someone following behind her*) We're just about to have coffee out here. If you'd care to join us . . .

(TRUDY *is followed by* DOUGLAS BEECHEY, *a man in his early forties. He is, as* JILL *has hinted, quite staggeringly unimpressive on first acquaintance. He is, though, as with many of nature's creatures, compensated for his apparent total lack of aggression by an almost complete invulnerability to attack by others. His clothes are quite unsuited to the climate.*)

DOUGLAS: (*As he approaches*) Isn't this glorious? Isn't this simply glorious . . . (*Stopping in the doorway to survey the patio and pool.*) Oh, now. This is glorious.

TRUDY: (*Unsure how to react*) Thank you. May I introduce (*indicating* KENNY) – have you met my husband's manager?

KENNY: (*Stepping towards them*) How do you do?

TRUDY: This is Kenneth Collins. Mr Beechey.

DOUGLAS: Douglas Beechey. How do you do?

KENNY: Kenny Collins. Good to meet you.

(*They shake hands.*)

DOUGLAS: Isn't this glorious? Isn't this just glorious? May I – (*He indicates the terrace.*)

TRUDY: (*Waving him in*) Of course.

DOUGLAS: (*Exploring the area*) Oh. Oh. Oh. Oh. (*Admiring the view from the garden gate.*) Oh. (*Investigating the pool.*) Oh. Look at this pool. Doesn't that look inviting?

TRUDY: You're welcome to have a swim, any time.

DOUGLAS: No, I don't swim.

TRUDY: No?

DOUGLAS: No, no. Me and water, I'm afraid, we've never seen eye to eye. (*Calling to the unseen* RUY) Hallo. Good morning to you.

TRUDY: I was just fetching another cup. Excuse me.

DOUGLAS: Of course. May I help at all . . .?

TRUDY: No, no. Wait there.

(TRUDY *goes back in to the house.*)

DOUGLAS: Well, I must say. Who could ask for anything more, eh?

KENNY: Yes.

DOUGLAS: Glorious. Quite glorious. (*Indicating in* RUY's *direction.*) Who's that? Is he one of the family?

KENNY: No, that's the gardener.

DOUGLAS: (*Impressed*) Oh. The gardener. I see.

KENNY: Right.

DOUGLAS: Very impressive. (*Looking around.*) All you need now is a garden, eh? (*He laughs.*)

KENNY: Well, I think he cleans the pool and – odd jobs, you know –

DOUGLAS: Oh, yes, I'm sure. I was only joking. I expect this paving would need weeding to start with. I should imagine. I suppose they get weeds here, don't they? Same as we do?

KENNY: I would imagine so.

DOUGLAS: (*Calling to* RUY) Excuse me, I say . . . Do you get weeds? I say! Do you have weeds here?

KENNY: I don't think he speaks much English.

DOUGLAS: Oh. (*Calling.*) Gracias! (*To* KENNY.) That's the only bit of Spanish I know.

9

KENNY: Pretty impressive.

DOUGLAS: I definitely don't know the Spanish for weed killer, that's for certain. (*Breathing in the air.*) Glorious! (*Slight pause.*)

KENNY: Good flight?

DOUGLAS: Pardon?

KENNY: Good flight? Out here? On the aeroplane? Did you have a good one?

DOUGLAS: Oh, glorious. I was with a very jolly crowd from Dagenham. Singing their heads off, all the way over.

KENNY: Oh, yes?

DOUGLAS: When they weren't playing practical jokes on the crew, that was. You had to laugh.

KENNY: Sounds fun.

DOUGLAS: Couple of them dressed up as air hostesses. Couple of the men. Then it turned out we were all staying in the same hotel. So . . .

KENNY: That OK? The hotel?

DOUGLAS: Very clean. And the windows open. That's all I ever ask for in a hotel.

KENNY: (*Slightly baffled*) Really?

DOUGLAS: I need air to sleep, you see. Not that I stay in them very often. Oh, I'm savouring every minute of this, I can tell you. Free trip. Free meals. Free hotel. VIP treatment. And appearing on the television. You don't get that every day, do you?

KENNY: You certainly don't.

DOUGLAS: Make the most of it, I say.

KENNY: I should.

DOUGLAS: I see they were all out there to greet my arrival. The film crew. I got to know them all quite well. While they were sitting in our front room for four days. Good to see them again. All out there. Filming away. And dear old Jill, waving her arms about as usual. She doesn't half go at them sometimes. Mind you, they take it all in very good part. They're a very pleasant bunch. Very easy-going, I've found. Well, let's put it this way, we certainly had a few good laughs while they were in Purley. (*He has moved back to stand by the garden gate*.) That'll be the Mediterranean Sea? Down there? Right?

KENNY: The bit covered in water. Where the land stops.

DOUGLAS: (*Surveying the view thoughtfully*) The Med, eh? Well, well. That's something else I can tell people I've seen. (TRUDY *returns with the extra cup*.)

TRUDY: Here we are.

DOUGLAS: Well, I can't say I'm not a tinge green, Mrs Parks. I must say, this is just perfection.

TRUDY: Yes, we're very – lucky.

KENNY: (*Anxious to correct any wrong impression*) Mind you, you didn't get it for nothing, did you? You've earned it.

DOUGLAS: (*Anxious to do the same*) Oh, yes.

TRUDY: Well, Vic earned it.

KENNY: You both have.

TRUDY: (*Smiling, unconvinced*) It's nice of you to say so.

DOUGLAS: Behind every successful man, don't they say?

TRUDY: I'm afraid my husband's still on the beach with the children. He should be back shortly.

DOUGLAS: Oh, how many children have you?

TRUDY: Two. Coffee, Mr Beechey?

DOUGLAS: Thank you. Do call me Douglas, won't you? Milk and three sugars, thank you.

TRUDY: Kenny?

KENNY: Please. Usual. Black, no sugar.

DOUGLAS: And how old are the children, Trudy – may I call you Trudy?

TRUDY: Cindy is seven and Timmy is just five.

DOUGLAS: Lovely. One of each, then?

TRUDY: Yes.

DOUGLAS: They must love it out here.

TRUDY: Oh, yes, they do. (*Offering him coffee*.) Mr Beechey.

DOUGLAS: Thank you. Douglas. Please. Call me Douglas. (*Slight pause.* KENNY *is served coffee*.)

KENNY: Thanks. Do you have children, Mr – Douglas?

DOUGLAS: No. No. (*A slight pause as if he might be going to say something else*.) No.

KENNY: Ah.

DOUGLAS: My wife was – Well, we made a joint decision not to have any. We decided we weren't ideal parent material. Either of us.

KENNY: It's a pity your wife couldn't come with you.

DOUGLAS: Oh, no. Nerys is not a traveller.

KENNY: No?

DOUGLAS: I'm afraid this sort of trip would be quite beyond her.

KENNY: Oh. What a shame.

(*Pause.*)

TRUDY: She's – She's all right, is she? I mean, she's not ill, your wife?

DOUGLAS: Oh, no. She's very chirpy.

KENNY: Oh, grand.

DOUGLAS: At present. She has her ups and downs, of course.

TRUDY: Don't we all?

KENNY: Absolutely.

(*Pause.*)

TRUDY: You'll appreciate that I'm Vic's second wife. I wasn't around when – when all that happened – I mean, Vic and I, we've only been married eight years.

DOUGLAS: Yes, I did read he'd remarried. I read all about your romance. In his book.

TRUDY: (*Not pleased*) Did you?

DOUGLAS: Sounded very romantic. Is that how it actually was? Did he really abduct you from the middle of a public car park in the back of a transit van?

TRUDY: (*Reluctantly*) Well, sort of, yes . . .

KENNY: Mind you, Trudy was standing around for some time waiting to be abducted, weren't you?

(DOUGLAS *laughs. Another pause.*)

TRUDY: No, what I'm saying is that – all that happened – all that – between you – happened while Vic was married to Donna, you see. I was not around then. I didn't even know him. I was married to somebody else as well, as it happens. Only that didn't work out.

DOUGLAS: That would be your previous marriage to the dental mechanic?

TRUDY: Yes . . .

DOUGLAS: Oh, dear . . .

TRUDY: (*Faintly irritated*) No, what I'm saying is, I had nothing to do with that part of Vic's life. If they want to know about that – for this programme – then they'll have to ask Donna. Providing they can sober her up. By the time I met Vic that was all in the past. I wasn't a part of it and I don't really want to know about it. We're all different people now. At least I hope we are. And I have to say that I don't agree with this programme anyway. I don't honestly think they should be doing it. I'm sorry. I've said it to Vic and I've said it to her. That Jill Rillington. And now I'm saying it to you. I'm sorry. I think it's unnecessary. And hurtful. I think it's raking over old ground and opening old wounds. I'm not at all surprised your wife isn't here. If I were her, I certainly wouldn't be here. Not after what she – Still. As I say, I'm an outsider. I wasn't even around when it happened. And what Vic does is his own affair. But I am his wife and I think I might have been consulted. I'm also the mother of his children – though you wouldn't think so sometimes, would you? (*She is suddenly on the verge of crying.*) Excuse me. I just have to fetch some – things . . .

(TRUDY *hurries into the house.* DOUGLAS *rises, amazed.* KENNY *remains seated.*)

KENNY: (*Calling calmly after her*) Trudy . . . love . . . (*Silence.*) She'll be all right.

DOUGLAS: Oh, dear. I had no idea she felt . . . I mean, I wouldn't . . .

KENNY: She'll be fine. Don't worry. Things are just a bit (*he gestures*) – you know . . .

DOUGLAS: How do you mean?

KENNY: Between them. Her and Vic.

DOUGLAS: Oh . . .

KENNY: Just at the moment. Temporarily. Nothing at all, really. Vic's a bit of a lad sometimes. I mean, I've known them both for ages. They're terrific people. Both of them. I should know. It was me who introduced them.

DOUGLAS: Did you really? That wasn't in the book.

KENNY: Vic was just – getting going, you know, after – after his leave of absence – and he took me on – initially as his agent – and later on, as he got in greater demand, I became his personal manager. I got him his first weekly TV slot – regional, mind you – sort of local *Crimewatch/Police Five* sort of thing, you know – scare the old ladies off to bed type of show – and Trudy was a friend of the producer's secretary or somesuch. And. Romance, romance.

DOUGLAS: I hope this programme hasn't created a tension between them.

KENNY: No, no, no . . . Why on earth should it? Nice plug for Vic. Nice holiday for you – as you say – all expenses paid. Who's it hurting? I mean, your wife didn't object, did she? And she has far more reason to than Trudy, hasn't she? But your wife's presumably perfectly happy for you to be here?

DOUGLAS: Well, Nerys had initial objections, I have to say. And she certainly didn't want to be any part of it herself. Although Jill Rillington did try very hard to persuade her to be interviewed. But Nerys said if I wanted to do it and Vic Parks wanted to do it, then who was she . . . I mean, the way Jill described the programme to me, I think it's a very interesting idea, don't you? What's happened to us all since. Since . . .

KENNY: Oh, you bet . . .

DOUGLAS: Take Vic, for instance. He has had the most amazing career, hasn't he? Considering.

KENNY: Oh, incredible . . .

DOUGLAS: I mean, from what he was then – to what he is now. He's an example to us all, isn't he?

KENNY: He is.

DOUGLAS: A remarkable man. You have to admire him. What he's done. Particularly for the young people. And all that from nothing.

KENNY: Less than that really.

DOUGLAS: Absolutely.

(*Slight pause.*)

KENNY: I suppose quite a lot must have happened to you, as well? In, what is it, seventeen years? You must have seen some changes in your own life.

14

DOUGLAS: One or two. (*He reflects.*) Not many really. I married Nerys, of course. And I changed my job. Well, I could hardly have continued at the bank.

KENNY: Memories too painful, were they?

DOUGLAS: No, no. But people used to come in just to stare at me, you know. While we were trying to conduct bank business. And Mr Marsh – that was my manager at the time – he's retired now to Bournemouth – he felt my presence was not conducive to normal, satisfactory banking practices and he offered to request a transfer for me to another district. But I couldn't in all conscience leave Purley – I was born and bred there, you see – so I left the bank altogether. And then, hey presto, I was lucky enough to land a job straightaway with a local firm of double-glazing consultants, and I've been book-keeping for them ever since. Not an earth-shattering tale, perhaps, but one with a happy ending none the less.

KENNY: And a success story, too. In its own way.

DOUGLAS: True. True. Nerys and I are both happy, anyway. That's the main thing.

KENNY: And you've both got your health and strength.

DOUGLAS: And we've both got our health and strength, precisely. Well, Nerys is sometimes . . . But it's mostly in her mind. I've told her she looks fine. She really does. Her face is fine.

KENNY: Why, she's not – is she – still disfigured, is she?

DOUGLAS: Oh, no, no, no. All there is – if you look very carefully, she's got the faintest traces of scar tissue, just around here (*he indicates the side of his face*) – but you really couldn't tell, I promise. He did a marvellous job, that surgeon. One of the best of his day, he was – he's dead now, alas. Died last year –

KENNY: Oh, sad . . .

DOUGLAS: But if she wears the make-up, it's undetectable. No one could tell.

KENNY: Fine, then . . .

DOUGLAS: The trouble is, Nerys won't always trouble with the make-up. She can't always be bothered. So then she goes out to the shops and people start staring at her – or she imagines they're staring at her anyway – I don't honestly think,

15

myself, they bother to give her a second look, if you want the truth, still . . . Then she comes home upset and she won't go out of the house for months on end. I've said to her, Nerys, if you'd only wear the make-up, you wouldn't have all this upset, would you?

KENNY: A lot of women wear make-up.

DOUGLAS: They do. I've told her that.

KENNY: Most women wear make-up.

DOUGLAS: Yes. I mean, this is a special make-up, it has to be said. It's slightly thicker than normal. But it's the same principle. It's like I imagine they must wear on the television. Like dancers must wear. I expect.

KENNY: Right.

DOUGLAS: I mean, if she was a man, I'd have understood her reluctance . . .

KENNY: Oh, yes. If you were a man you wouldn't necessarily want to go strolling about in make-up, would you?

DOUGLAS: Not in Purley you wouldn't, certainly. But a woman.

(JILL *comes on through the garden gate. She is evidently angry.*)

JILL: Sod them. They are useless. They are worse than useless.

DOUGLAS: (*Rising*) Hallo, Jill . . .

JILL: (*Grimly*) Hallo, Mr Beechey. We may have to ask you to arrive all over again. We were just a little slow catching you first time around . . .

DOUGLAS: Right-oh, Jill. Just say the word. (*To* KENNY) I'm getting rather expert at this filming. She had me walking in and out of our kitchen, must have been thirty-five times one day. (*Laughingly to* JILL.) It was about that, wasn't it?

JILL: (*Unamused*) At least thirty-five. Is this coffee?

KENNY: Help yourself. Trudy's just – just . . . doing something or other.

(JILL *helps herself to coffee.*)

DOUGLAS: I did a very good sprint round the local park for you, though, didn't I? We got that in one take, didn't we? I'm looking forward to seeing that. I ran for miles, Kenneth, you've no idea. Nearly killed me. Go on, the crew kept shouting, keep going. (*He laughs.*) I'm looking forward to that.

16

JILL: Well, we may have to leave that bit out, Mr Beechey –

DOUGLAS: Oh, dear.

JILL: We've got so much wonderful stuff already.

DOUGLAS: The crew will be disappointed. It was their idea, wasn't it?

JILL: Yes. (*Beaming at him with her best professional smile.*) Anyway. You're here. That's the main thing. What are your first impressions then, Mr Beechey? Of this place?

KENNY: Glorious.

JILL: (*Irritably*) What?

DOUGLAS: Quite right. Glorious. I couldn't have put it better myself. I must say, I've always heard tell of the dazzling world of show business, but this is the first time I've ever experienced it.

JILL: You wouldn't mind it yourself?

DOUGLAS: I certainly wouldn't.

JILL: How do you feel about someone like, say, Vic having it?

DOUGLAS: Lucky him, that's what I say.

JILL: You don't feel it's wrong that he should have something like this and you don't?

DOUGLAS: I'm sorry, I don't quite follow, how do you mean? Is that a socialist question . . .?

KENNY: What are you trying to get him to say, Jilly?

DOUGLAS: Because I'm not a socialist. Actually, I'm not quite sure what I am just at present. The past few years I have been consciously withholding my vote –

JILL: So you don't feel just a little bit jealous?

DOUGLAS: Certainly not.

JILL: Not the teeniest bit?

DOUGLAS: No.

JILL: Honestly?

KENNY: Jill, the man's just said, he's not jealous –

DOUGLAS: (*Cheerfully*) Oh, don't worry. She's always going on at me like this . . .

JILL: I'm sorry, I simply cannot believe that after what happened Mr Beechey can sit here among all this – wealth – these spoils of the good life –

KENNY: Come on, Jilly, it's one poky, run-of-the-mill villa in the middle of hundreds – it's no big deal –

JILL: Maybe not to you or Vic or me it isn't. But to someone like Mr Beechey, it's beyond his wildest dreams . . .

KENNY: What are you talking about? This place is littered with people like Mr Beechey –

DOUGLAS: Do call me Douglas, please . . .

KENNY: The place is populated by Mr Beecheys. You can barely move for Beecheys, don't talk nonsense.

JILL: (*Angrily indicating* DOUGLAS) If you had seen – If you had seen, by contrast, the dingy little house this man is forced to live in. On the edge of a roaring main trunk road – rooms the size of this table – fading wallpaper . . . worn carpets . . . God! (*She shudders.*) Sorry, Mr Beechey, but . . .

DOUGLAS: (*Without offence*) We're really both quite fond of it, actually.

JILL: (*Calming down*) Just don't try and kid me he wouldn't prefer this if he were given a choice . . .

KENNY: And all I'm saying is, don't hold this place up as some fantastic dream palace. It's a perfectly ordinary holiday shack. A lot of people have one. Most people have one. If they've bothered to save up . . .

(*Slight pause.*)

DOUGLAS: Mind you, I think we've got used to that house over the years. You don't notice the little drawbacks quite so much after a while. I must be honest, we have meant to do something about that hall carpet for some years. But it's getting a good match with the stairs, you see. That's the problem. They don't really make that mauve any more. It means I have to keep bringing the samples home with me – because, of course, Nerys can't face walking into Debenhams, certainly not on a Saturday morning.

(*A silence.*)

KENNY: The man is just not the jealous type, Jill, forget it.

JILL: (*With ill-concealed annoyance*) So you have no feelings at all about this place, Mr Beechey? Like you appear not to have feelings about anything very much?

DOUGLAS: Oh, I have feelings, Jill, I most certainly do. Very deep feelings. But I sincerely hope that envy is not one of them. Because envy in my book is a deadly sin and as a practising Christian, that is something I try to avoid.

JILL: Super. I'm glad to hear it. Well, perhaps you ought to tell me something you do feel strongly about and we'll try and include that in the programme.

KENNY: Jill, come on . . .

JILL: Illegal parking on double yellow lines? Any good? Dogs fouling footpaths? Free double glazing for senior citizens?

DOUGLAS: (*Thoughtfully*) I suppose evil, really.

JILL: Evil?

DOUGLAS: Yes. I feel strongly about that.

JILL: That's it? Just evil?

DOUGLAS: Yes. Only, it's often hard to recognize. But there's a lot of it about, you know.

(*A silence. Suddenly, there in the garden gateway stands* VIC PARKS. *A powerful man in his late forties. He has just come from the beach and is wearing shorts, sports shirt and canvas beach shoes. Holding shyly on to his hand is his elder child* CINDY, *a pretty little girl of seven. The others don't immediately see him.*)

VIC: Good morning. Don't we say good morning, then?

(JILL *and* DOUGLAS *rise.* KENNY *follows suit, rather more slowly.*)

JILL: (*Delightedly*) Vic . . .

DOUGLAS: (*Obediently*) Good morning . . .

KENNY: (*With them*) About time . . .

VIC: (*Gently*) Cindy, you get changed and then you take Timmy up the other end of the pool, all right? And look after him, OK?

(CINDY *runs off again.*)

(*Shouting after her*) And do what Sharon says. You listen to Sharon, all right?

JILL: (*Embracing him*) Hallo, Vic.

VIC: Hallo, how's my girl?

JILL: Grateful you've decided to turn up.

VIC: Well, where are the cameras, then? Where're the cameras? I thought this place would be a mass of people. Cameras, sound men, extra lighting rigs . . . Look at it, I ask you. Bugger all. I make my special entrance. Get dressed up specially . . .

JILL: I sent them off to do the mute shots. They'll be back in an hour –

VIC: They'd better be. I came all the way up from the beach for this – (*To* DOUGLAS) How do you do, Vic Parks. You'll be –

JILL: This is Douglas Beechey –

DOUGLAS: Hallo. Great to meet you. I'm a real fan –

VIC: Well, that's very nice to hear. (*To* JILL) Listen, you'll get the kids in somewhere, won't you? Just one shot, eh?

JILL: Oh, sure . . .

VIC: Only I promised Timmy and Cindy they'd be on the telly, you see . . .

JILL: I was hoping you would let us use them . . .

VIC: Just one shot. (*To* DOUGLAS.) Have you got kids?

DOUGLAS: No, no. But I watch your programme. I watch *Ask Vic* every Tuesday –

VIC: (*To* KENNY) Now, isn't that interesting? Here's another example . . .

(RUY, *who has finished raking the swimming pool, has entered and is crossing to the back gate.*)

Morning, Ruy, lad –

RUY: (*Cheerily animated*) Hallo, good morning, Mr Vic!

VIC: (*To* JILL *and* DOUGLAS) You know, they did a survey as to what categories of kids make up the viewing sample for *Ask Vic* and they actually found that – 15 per cent, wasn't it?

KENNY: Thirteen and a half –

VIC: Nearly 15 per cent of our viewers were adults over the age of twenty-one –

KENNY: Age of eighteen –

VIC: Isn't that incredible?

DOUGLAS: Incredible.

VIC: No, you think about it for a minute. That's a big percentage, that is, 15 per cent.

DOUGLAS: Amazing.

VIC: Whereas my evening show – *The Vic Parks Show* – that is exclusively adult. Well, point oh-one per cent kids, or something. So there's no cross spill the other way. Which I find very interesting.

KENNY: It is on at eleven o'clock at night, of course –

VIC: No. Even so.

DOUGLAS: Yes, it's a bit late for me, that one . . .

VIC: What, early riser, are you? (*Claps him on the back.*) Nothing like it. We were down there at what, six thirty this morning. Magic. Best time to be on a beach. First thing in the morning. Virgin sand, sun coming up, not too hot, clear blue sea . . . Now, have you all got what you want? Drink? Food? Anything? Where's Trudy? Isn't she looking after you? I told her to look after you. (*Calling into the house.*) Trudy! Where is she?

KENNY: Trudy's just –

(SHARON GIFFIN *has entered from the garden gate. A girl of about nineteen. Overweight and sadly graceless. She is at present in a sulk. She carries a couple of baskets with towels, toys, etc., which presumably they've brought back from the beach. She is wearing a wetsuit top under her beach robe.*)

VIC: Sharon, find Trudy. Tell her to come out here.

SHARON: (*Flatly*) Yes, Mr Parks.

DOUGLAS: (*To* SHARON) Hallo, I'm Douglas.

SHARON: (*All but ignoring him*) Hallo.

(SHARON *goes into the house.*)

JILL: We're being looked after fine, Vic. You don't have to worry about us –

VIC: No, I can't stand guests being left on their own. That's terrible. I can't stand that. (*Feeling the coffee pot.*) This is cold and all. (*Yelling.*) Marta! Marta! Sitting here drinking cold coffee. What the hell's going on here? Marta! Come out here. Sit down. Go on. Sit down.

(*They sit.* MARTA, *a Spanish woman in her fifties, enters in a hurry from the house. Normally dark and brooding but, as with her husband* RUY, *in the presence of* VIC *she is effusive and charming.*)

MARTA: Yes, Mr Vic?

VIC: Marta, coffee. More coffee. Hot. More cups. Clean. Quickly. All right?

MARTA: (*Taking the tray from the table*) More coffee, more cups.

VIC: Hot coffee. Understand?

MARTA: Hot coffee.

21

VIC: Hot not cold.

MARTA: (*Hurrying away*) Hot not cold. Yes, Mr Vic.

> (MARTA *goes.* VIC *sits at last, like someone about to hold court.*
> DOUGLAS *is holding his old coffee cup. The occasional child's
> shout is heard from the direction of the swimming pool.*)

VIC: Now then – that's sorted that out . . . (*Seeing the children.*)
Look at those two. Look at those kids.

DOUGLAS: (*Smiling appreciatively*) Ah . . .

VIC: You got kids, have you?

DOUGLAS: Er – no . . .

VIC: Have some. You don't know what you're missing.
(*Indicating Douglas's cup.*) Leave that, she's fetching some
more –
> (DOUGLAS *puts his cup down again, obediently.*)
> (*Indicating* KENNY) I'm always telling him that. Kenny. He
should have some.

KENNY: (*Uneasily*) Well, it's tricky . . .

JILL: Kenny's gay, Vic. He doesn't want kids.

VIC: Why not? What obstacle's that? These days? Being a poof?

KENNY: Quite a bit actually. Anyway, I hate kids, I loathe the
sight of them.

VIC: (*To* JILL) You should have some, too.

JILL: No, thanks. I'll enjoy other people's kids. Much nicer.

VIC: (*Only just joking*) It's unnatural not to. Every woman who
can should have kids. Like every man who can should grow a
beard. Everything you can do you ought to do. Before you
die. That's what we're here for. Right?

JILL: Tell you what, I'll grow my armpits and you have the baby,
OK?

VIC: (*Mock disgusted*) Dear, oh, dear. Right. What's the plan? (*To*
JILL.) You're going to make us two into telly stars, are you?
(*He winks at* DOUGLAS. DOUGLAS *laughs appreciatively.*)

JILL: I thought the best way to go about this, Vic – with your
approval, of course – is this morning, as soon as the boys
come back, I'll pick up one or two mute shots here. But
perhaps we could spend now, we three, just briefly talking
about what we want to talk about. And then this afternoon –
(*She hesitates as* VIC *rises and moves towards the house.*)

This after—

VIC: Carry on, Jill. Carry on, I'm listening . . .

JILL: (*Having to shout rather as* VIC *disappears*) This afternoon, I could start by talking with the two of you, just to contrast how you've both fared over seventeen years —

VIC: (*Off, calling*) Trudy! Trudy! (*Calling back to* JILL.) Seventeen years, yes, I'm listening . . .

JILL: (*Battling on*) And perhaps — I don't want to dwell on it too much — perhaps just recalling the last meeting between you both —

VIC: (*Off*) Where are my bloody cigars?

TRUDY: (*Off*) They're in the drawer, there.

VIC: (*Off*) They are not in the drawer.

TRUDY: (*Off*) Well, they were there.

VIC: (*Off*) Look at that. Look. Is that in the drawer? Is that what's meant by in the drawer?

TRUDY: (*Off*) Oh, I know where they are, just a minute . . .

VIC: (*Off*) Well, bring them out here. We're trying to talk out here. Come on out. (VIC *re-enters from the house*.) Sorry, Jilly, sorry. I apologize. Carry on. (JILL *opens her mouth to do so*.) No, sorry, excuse me — before you do, let me say — Doug — Duggie — can I call you Doug?

DOUGLAS: (*Delighted*) Yes, of course —

VIC: Doug — this girl — discovered me. Can you believe that? This little kid — ankle socks — how old were you, then? Seventeen, something like that —

JILL: (*Rather coyly*) I was older than that . . .

KENNY: Twenty-three, you were twenty-three when you met Vic —

JILL: Something like that.

VIC: This girl — she was — what? You were a local radio interviewer, weren't you?

JILL: Right.

VIC: I'd just — like, come out, you know — and she's doing this programme about — what was it? *Old Lags' Hour* or something, wasn't it?

(VIC *winks at* DOUGLAS. DOUGLAS *laughs appreciatively. The whole of the following gets related rather for his benefit*.)

23

No, seriously, it was a programme called – let me see
Facing Things – right?

KENNY: *Facing Up*, it was called.

JILL: *Facing Up*.

VIC: *Facing Up*, he's right –

JILL: About long-term prisoners coming to terms –

VIC: With the outside world . . .

JILL: And this man, his first time on radio –

VIC: The very first time I'd ever been on, this is –

JILL: By the time we'd finished I'd got enough tape for about
twenty-five programmes . . .

VIC: And then when I'm leaving – you left out the best bit – just
when I'm leaving, wasn't it?

JILL: Oh, yes, right – and then just as he's leaving – leaving the
studio – I'm absolutely exhausted by now, mind you – and
he turns to me and he says –

VIC: (*Laughing*) I said to her, what about my book then?

JILL: He says, you never asked me about my book.
(JILL, VIC *and* KENNY *laugh.* DOUGLAS *joins in, though it's
clear he doesn't know what they're all laughing about.*)
He's only written a bloody book as well . . .

VIC: *My Life* by Vic Parks. Written during Her Majesty's
Pleasure – and on Her Majesty's stationery.

KENNY: (*To* DOUGLAS) His biography.

DOUGLAS: Oh, yes . . .

KENNY: The first one, that was –

VIC: The authorized version. It was a shocker, wasn't it?

KENNY: Not the one you've read –

VIC: No, that's the second one he must have read.

KENNY: That was *Life as a Straight Man*.

VIC: That only came out a year ago.

KENNY: Eighteen months –

DOUGLAS: It seemed to be very popular at the library. There
was quite a waiting list at the Purley Branch –

VIC: Five months at number one . . . Can't be bad.

DOUGLAS: And you wrote that yourself? I mean, that was
actually yourself writing, was it?

VIC: Er, more or less. More or less. They were mostly my

words. That's fair to say, isn't it?

KENNY: That's no lie.

VIC: There was just – someone else putting them in the right order for me.

KENNY: A little bit of help from John.

VIC: A little bit of help from John. Bless him. How is he, by the way?

KENNY: Much better.

VIC: Good. Good. Give him my love.

(TRUDY *comes out with a box of cigars and some matches.*)

TRUDY: Here you are.

VIC: Ta. Sit down, sit down.

TRUDY: No, I –

VIC: Sit down. We're just remembering my first book. Did you ever read that?

TRUDY: (*Sitting, rather reluctantly*) No, I never read that one.

VIC: (*To* JILL) It was a shocker, wasn't it? I don't know how I had the nerve to show it –

JILL: Don't knock it, now. That started you off, that book.

VIC: No, that was you, my darling. You started me off.

KENNY: She recognized star quality . . .

VIC: It was no thanks to that bloody book. I tried that, you know, with – must have been twenty-five publishers –

JILL: But it was you reading that book that started your career. I mean, if some producer hadn't heard you reading it on *Pick of the Week*, you'd never have got on *Start the Week*. And if you hadn't done *Start the Week* they'd never have asked you to do *Stop the Week*, would they?

KENNY: Or *Any Questions* . . .

VIC: (*Modestly*) True.

KENNY: Or *The Book Programme*. Or *Did you See . . .*?

VIC: True, true . . .

KENNY: And the rest is history . . .

JILL: Absolutely true.

(*Pause, whilst they all consider* VIC's *mercurial rise to fame.*
MARTA *comes out with a tray of fresh coffee and five cups.*
TRUDY *pours coffee during the next.* MARTA *hovers behind her.*
The sound of the children's shouts from the far end of the pool.)

25 .

VIC: (*Shouting to them*) Be careful now. Be careful, Cindy. Now, don't push him.

TRUDY: Are they all right?

VIC: They're all right.

TRUDY: Where's Sharon? Shouldn't she be with them?

VIC: She's getting changed, I think.

TRUDY: She should be with them . . .

VIC: They're all right. Don't fuss. I'm keeping an eye on them. (*To* DOUGLAS.) You got kids, did you say?

DOUGLAS: No . . .

VIC: You like them, though?

DOUGLAS: Oh, yes . . .

VIC: Look at them. Look at those two . . . I love kids. Do you know what I'd do to people who hurt kids?

DOUGLAS: No.

VIC: I'd sit them, naked, astride barbed wire . . .

DOUGLAS: (*Wincing slightly*) Ah . . .

TRUDY: (*Irritated by* MARTA's *presence behind her*) Thank you, Marta, I can manage, thank you.

VIC: No, let her serve round. She's waiting to serve round, Trudy . . .

TRUDY: I can serve round.

VIC: No, let her. That's her job. That's what she's paid for. We're paying her to serve round. (*To* MARTA.) Go on. Serve round, you silly cow. Serve them round.

MARTA: (*A flashing smile*) Yes, Mr Vic.

VIC: We're paying her. We might as well use the bloody woman. Like buying a light bulb and sitting in the dark otherwise, isn't it?

(VIC *winks at* DOUGLAS. DOUGLAS *laughs rather more weakly.* TRUDY *has poured out all the coffee and, during the next,* MARTA *circulates with the tray, allowing the guests to serve themselves with cream and sugar.*)

Anyway. (*To* JILL.) You still haven't told us, sweetheart, have you, what your grand plan of campaign is. We await your plan.

JILL: Well, I was trying to –

VIC: (*About to light a cigar*) Cigar, anyone? Cigar? (*They decline.*)

26

Sorry, excuse me, carry on.

JILL: I thought that the three of us could do an initial three-handed interview this afternoon. Out here, if that's OK –

VIC: What? You, me and him, you mean?

JILL: Right.

VIC: Right. Carry on.

JILL: I'd like to use that to discuss, principally, how both your lives have changed over seventeen years –

VIC: How long have you got? (*He laughs.*)

JILL: Well, it'll have to be in general terms . . .

VIC: It'll need to be . . .

TRUDY: Excuse me, but why are you going back seventeen years? I mean, if you're talking about Vic's career, that only started eight years ago –

VIC: It started the day I met you, my love . . .

(VIC *winks at* DOUGLAS *again.*)

TRUDY: (*Unamused*) No, I mean it. Why are you wanting to go back seventeen years? I don't see any reason to.

JILL: Because – (*As if talking to a child.*) That's the point of the programme, Trudy. That's the name of the series, *Their Paths Crossed.* And seventeen years ago, that's when their paths crossed. These two. Douglas and Vic.

TRUDY: Yes, I know. I just don't see why you have to go back through all that again. All that business in the bank – the trial –

JILL: We're not. Not really –

VIC: We are certainly not. Let's get that clear.

TRUDY: (*Clearly upset*) I don't see any point in dragging all that up again. We've got the kids growing up. A new life. Why do you want to talk about it, for heaven's sake . . .?

VIC: (*Sharply to her*) Trudy! Listen, we're not going to talk about it, all right? (*Pause.*) Look, I think, actually, Trudy, in this instance, is right. We don't need to go back seventeen years, do we?

TRUDY: No, we don't.

VIC: It's pointless. I mean, I was inside for the first nine, so what's the point?

TRUDY: There's no point.

JILL: But seventeen years ago is when you met Mr Beechey.
That's when your paths crossed. As a result of which, his life
changed, your life changed.
VIC: His life might have done. Mine didn't. I just went back to
prison. That was nothing new to me then, I can tell you . . .
JILL: Well, it certainly changed Mr Beechey's life –
VIC: Well, do a programme about him, then. I don't mind.
JILL: No, listen –
KENNY: Vic, I think what Jill's saying is that that's the point of
the programme. I mean, unless you do trace back to when
you both met –
VIC: No. Bugger it. I don't want to go back that far. Trudy's
right. What's the point?
TRUDY: No point at all.
VIC: Anyway, it's all in my book. If you want it, it's all there in
the book.
TRUDY: It wouldn't have been in that, either, if I'd had my way.
JILL: (*Trying to control her anger*) Well, terrific. (Pause.) You're
not prepared to talk about the bank raid at all, then?
VIC: Sorry, no. It's been done to death.
JILL: Not like this it hasn't. (*Pause. JILL can see her programme
disappearing.*) Not even in general detail?
VIC: What do you mean, in general detail?
JILL: I mean, just a general description of what happened. In very
general terms. Look, I do appreciate that it isn't easy for
either of you –
(*No one speaks.*)
I don't intend to go into any great lurid details. I was just
planning to have both your voices speaking over a simple
reconstruction – using posed actors in still pictures – I must
stress that – I'm using stills, not even live action – I don't
want anything sensational – God forbid – it's not a
sensational slot, it can't be, it's scheduled for eight o'clock.
That's all there would be. Just your voices over still pictures.
Telling it as you remembered it. (*She stops and looks at them,
awaiting response.*) I mean, none of what I'm saying is exactly
new, you know. I did say all this to you, Kenneth.
Originally. Months ago, Last November. Didn't I?

28

KENNY: (*Vaguely*) Yes. I know, it's just . . . Obviously, if Vic feels . . . (*He tails off.*)

VIC: (*Indicating* DOUGLAS) Does he want to talk about this? You want all this dragged up again, Doug?

DOUGLAS: Well . . . I can see both points of view, really –

JILL: Listen, the bulk of the programme, 99.999 per cent of it – I promise – is about what happened afterwards. About how you became a TV personality with an umpteen-million viewing figure –

KENNY: Nine million.

VIC: (*To* KENNY) Are we down to nine? Since when are we down to nine?

KENNY: Only for last week.

VIC: Why?

KENNY: Motor show.

VIC: Oh.

JILL: (*Sensing a victory*) I think one of the fascinating things is the way both your careers have reversed, in a sense. I mean, seventeen years ago, Mr Beechey here was a national hero. Just looking at these press cuttings . . . (*She opens her folder.*) One newspaper actually started the Beechey Awards – given annually to anyone having a go at criminals. Isn't that right?

DOUGLAS: Yes, they did. I presented them myself the first year. At The Grosvenor House. A very splendid do.

JILL: (*Rifling through the cuttings*) 'Get that Beechey spirit, Britain' . . . 'We will fight them on the Beecheys' . . . 'Beechey's the boy for us'. (*Examining a press photograph.*) Who are all these women with you, incidentally?

DOUGLAS: Do you know, I never really found out. They just turned up in a coach one morning. With the photographer. We all got very chilly, I recall. Especially them.

VIC: (*Examining the cutting*) Dear, oh, dear. (*Showing it to* TRUDY) Look at that . . . Disgraceful. (*He tuts with mock horror.*)

JILL: But, looking at all these press cuttings, I wonder who'd remember you now?

DOUGLAS: Oh, no one at all, I shouldn't think.

JILL: So heroes do get forgotten?

DOUGLAS: I think ones like me do.

KENNY: (*Studying one of the cuttings*) How long did they keep up these Beechey Awards?

DOUGLAS: Oh, three years. Then the paper went on to something else. Raising money for the Olympic Games, I think.

JILL: Rather sad, don't you think?

VIC: No, that's life. Human nature. I mean, for the public, it's on to the next, isn't it? Has to be. Only natural.

JILL: Only this particular hero was eventually to be replaced by the very man he so gallantly risked his life having a go at in the first place. A man who had fired a shotgun into an innocent girl's face –

TRUDY: Listen, if we're going to start on that –

VIC: (*Sharply*) Trudy, sit down . . .

(TRUDY *sits. Silence.*)

(*Quietly*) Now that is an oversimplified statement and out of order, Jill. And you know it. Now, I'm prepared to do your interview – I've said I would, so I will – I'm prepared to do all I can to help you with your programme – but not if we're going to have semi-libellous statements chucked about the place, all right?

JILL: I don't see your objections. Everybody knows you shot her. As you say, it's in your book. So what's the mystery?

TRUDY: Because we're trying to forget it –

JILL: If he's trying to forget it, why is he making money writing books about it?

KENNY: No, that's totally unfair –

VIC: Ten per cent of all my royalties from that book are going to recognized children's charities –

JILL: (*Riding over this*) Why's he got a kids' programme on television and a chat show at weekends?

KENNY: Because, put at its simplest, Vic has a personality which the public at large warm to and want to watch –

JILL: They watch him because he used to be a bank robber. That's why they watch him.

KENNY: That's total and complete bollocks – excuse me – none of the kids who watch Vic have the faintest idea what he used to be –

JILL: Yes, they have –

KENNY: They weren't even born –

JILL: Yes, they have because he tells them. Listen to me, kids, I went down the wrong street once and believe me, tangling with the law is strictly for mugs –

VIC: Now, hold on. Hold on. Be fair –

KENNY: Do you realize the number of kids this man has kept out of prison . . .?

JILL: I've no doubt he has –

KENNY: There have been surveys done amongst underprivileged kids –

JILL: I'm sure. I'm not saying Vic isn't doing a wonderful job. He is. Of course he is. All I'm saying is – all I'm saying – (*She hesitates.*)

TRUDY: (*Coolly*) What exactly are you saying? Exactly?

JILL: All I'm saying is – isn't it ironic that the hero is forgotten? And the villain has now become the hero. That's all. And isn't that a reflection of our time?

TRUDY: Fascinating.

JILL: And whilst we're saying it, isn't it even more tragic that the person who lost most in all this – the victim herself – no one spares a thought for her at all. Except Douglas, of course.

TRUDY: (*Muttering*) I knew we'd get round to this . . .

VIC: If you think I didn't spend nine years of my life thinking about that girl, then you don't know me – that's all I can say. I have woken in the night – (*To* TRUDY) I still do occasionally – don't I? In a sweat, wringing wet, still remembering it. So don't you come at me with that one. I paid –

TRUDY: Vic –

VIC: No, let me finish – I paid the full penalty as prescribed by the law for what I did. In full. Fourteen years less remission – nine years. And that to me has to mean a debt paid in full. Otherwise what more can a man do? Eh? Go on blaming himself? What's the point of that?

TRUDY: No point.

VIC: None. He has got to get up and do the very best with that which God has granted him to make amends with and try and put something back in the world, in the brief time left to him. And that is what, hand on heart, I have tried to do. Bear me out, Kenny, is that not what I have tried to do . . .?

KENNY: Absolutely, Vic.

VIC: Right. (*To* JILL.) Jill, there is no use in going back over the past where no one is going to benefit. It's not going to help me. (*Indicating* DOUGLAS.) It's not going to help him. And it's certainly not going to help that poor bloody bitch who was injured – sorry, she's your wife, mate, I shouldn't refer to her like that . . . It's not going to help her either . . .

TRUDY: Not in the least.

KENNY: Absolutely not.

(*Pause.*)

VIC: I mean, you talk about villains, you talk about heroes. But what is that? It's very often a value judgement made by society, which has no basis in fact whatsoever. I mean, has it?

JILL: I don't know. You tell me.

VIC: Well, I'm telling you. It hasn't. I mean, take that instance. I'm cast as the villain, right? Because it just so happens that on that particular occasion it was me who happened to be the one who walked into the bank with a shotgun with the intention of robbing it. Another day, another time, another set of circumstances, it could have been someone else, couldn't it? Could have been you. Could have been him. Now, I'm not pretending that what I did was a right course of action – But. But, let's add these factors. I had no intention at any stage of using that firearm. It was on my previous record for all to see that I never used a firearm, I never condoned the use of firearms. I detest firearms. Even now – Well, we did a programme on firearms the other day, didn't we, Kenny? Kenny here will vouch for me, I couldn't even bring myself to pick one up, could I? And if you will care to check, and it is on record from sworn witnesses at the trial, the very first words I said when the three of us first came through those bank doors, my first words were: 'All right. Don't get excited and nobody'll get injured.' (*To* DOUGLAS.) You were there. Did I not say those exact words?

DOUGLAS: Nobody'll get hurt. Don't get excited and nobody'll get hurt, you said . . .

VIC: There you are. Would I have said that if I'd come in there to shoot somebody?

JILL: But the gun was loaded –

VIC: Well, yes, it was loaded. What's the point of carrying an empty gun?

JILL: So you knew you might use it?

VIC: (*Sharply*) I've said I had no intention of using it, all right? Is my word not good enough?
(*A pause.*)

DOUGLAS: The safety catch was off, though.

VIC: (*Irritably*) What?

DOUGLAS: I said, the safety catch was off. I remember the police saying so at the time.

VIC: Well, of course it was. Look, come on, be fair. You cannot walk into a bank with a gun and expect people to take you seriously if you've still got the safety on, can you?

JILL: Why not?

VIC: (*Angrily*) Because people aren't going to take much notice of you for a kick off, are they? All they're going to say is, this geezer's an idiot, he's wandering round with his safety on . . .

JILL: Most people would never know the difference, would they? I wouldn't know if a safety catch was on or off.

VIC: Maybe you wouldn't. But some people would, that's all I'm saying . . .

JILL: You mean other bank robbers?

VIC: Look, there's plenty of people besides bank robbers who use shotguns, you know. I mean, a lot of people use shotguns. People working in the bank, they probably use shotguns –

JILL: What, in the bank?

VIC: At the weekend. They probably use shotguns.

JILL: Do you use one?

DOUGLAS: No, I never use shotguns.

VIC: Not him. I'm not talking about him. I mean, the managers. As a matter of fact, I think my manager shoots. (*To* KENNY.) David shoots, doesn't he? David?

KENNY: No, I think he water-skis.

VIC: No. Well, there are some. Take my word for it. Anyway, the

33

point I am making is, responsible as I may have been – and I've never denied that – for carrying a gun into that place (*Indicating* DOUGLAS), if this one hadn't come at me – if this six-and-a-half-stone boy-scout bank clerk hadn't come charging at me from the length of the bank – I would never have fired . . .

JILL: You're not saying it was Mr Beechey's fault, are you?

VIC: No. I'm not saying that. But if he hadn't been a hero, if he hadn't grabbed me, the gun would never have gone off accidentally and this girl would never have got hurt. I mean, as it was, he was clinging on – I was shouting – 'Be careful, it'll go off, it'll go off' – and I could see, you know, this girl was in the firing line –

JILL: She was the one you'd been holding as a hostage?

VIC: Yes, originally. But I'd released her in order to wrestle with him. As soon as I appreciated the danger, I let her go. I could see, though, as he and I were struggling, that the gun was twisting round towards her – (*To* DOUGLAS) You had your back to her, so you couldn't have seen – and I was trying, you know, to pull it back away from her – and then, before I can do anything to stop it, bang – Right in the side of her face. It was a miracle, with the gun that close, she didn't lose an eye. A miracle. I thank God for that, at least.
(*A respectful pause.*)

DOUGLAS: She did lose her ear, though.

VIC: Well, yes. Still. An ear's not the same as eye, is it?

KENNY: I suppose she could grow her hair . . .

DOUGLAS: Yes, she did.

VIC: She's all right now, then, is she?

DOUGLAS: Oh, yes. She's pretty chirpy. Has her ups and downs, of course.

TRUDY: Like most of us.

VIC: Lovely girl.

DOUGLAS: Yes, she was.

KENNY: Lucky man.

DOUGLAS: Yes, she was beautiful.

JILL: She still is. From what I saw of her, anyway.

VIC: She's not in the film?

34

JILL: No.

DOUGLAS: I think she'd have found it difficult –

VIC: Oh, yes.

JILL: And, anyway, as I keep saying, this programme is really about you two. Not her at all. I don't want it to be macabre or morbid or cause a lot of unnecessary pain – I mean, frankly, I'm not into that sort of programme, I'm sorry. I mean, I know some people make careers out of it, we've all seen them, they love to have the camera lingering over people crying and obviously in terrible distress, but I'm sorry, I find that simply gratuitous and tasteless. That's not what I'm here to do. And if that means I'm into old-fashioned programme values, then you'll have to forgive me.

VIC: Hear! Hear! You and me both, baby. (*Pause.*) So is that it, then? Are we excused? Only I think I fancy a swim.

TRUDY: Just a minute. Have you agreed to talk about the robbery or not?

JILL: Only very, very, very briefly. I need to a little, just to establish the programme.

TRUDY: Well, it had better be briefly.

VIC: It'll be brief, don't worry. It's old news, anyway. Who's interested? (*Indicating* DOUGLAS.) He doesn't want it dragged up, I don't want it dragged up. His wife certainly doesn't. So that's the end of it. You fancy a swim, Doug?

DOUGLAS: Er, no . . .

VIC: Before we have a drink . . .

DOUGLAS: No, me and water, I'm afraid, I –

TRUDY: (*In sudden alarm*) Timmy! (TRUDY *rushes off to the far end of the swimming pool.* Cindy, hold on to him! (VIC *moves towards the pool after* TRUDY.)

JILL: (*Seeing what's happening*) Oh, my God.

VIC: Have you got him?

TRUDY: (*Off*) You naughty boy. Don't ever do that again. (*Calling*) Yes, he's all right. My God, he nearly went in. (*To* TIMMY.) Now, I told you before . . .

(JILL, KENNY *and* DOUGLAS *have risen to watch.*)

KENNY: That was a close thing.

JILL: He's all right, though.

DOUGLAS: Could have been nasty . . .

> (SHARON *appears from the house. She has changed into her swimsuit. She stops to watch the commotion.*)

SHARON: What's happening?

JILL: Timmy nearly fell in. Weren't you supposed to be keeping an eye on them?

SHARON: I just went to change – (*Calling.*) Is he all right?

> (VIC *turns from the pool and looks at* SHARON.)

VIC: (*Beckoning* SHARON) Hey, come here.

SHARON: What?

VIC: Here. Come here.

> (SHARON *crosses obediently over to him.* VIC *speaks to her quietly, but not so quietly that the others cannot hear him.*)
> Where the bloody hell have you been, eh?

SHARON: Pardon, Mr Parks . . .

VIC: (*Very close to her*) My kid was practically drowned, and where were you? Eh?

SHARON: (*Frightened*) I was changing, Mr Parks . . .

VIC: Changing? I see. You were changing while my child was nearly drowning. That's your idea of looking after them, is it? Is it?

SHARON: (*With a reflex smile due to pure nervousness*) No.

VIC: I hope you're not laughing about this, girl, because I'm not. Are you laughing? It's a joke to you, is it? Is it a joke?

> (SHARON *can't reply. She shakes her head.*)
> Do you hear what I'm saying to you? I'm asking you, do you think it's a joke? Do you?

JILL: Vic . . .

VIC: I'm waiting to hear from you. Do you think it's a joke?

SHARON: (*Tearful now*) No, Mr Parks.

VIC: Good. I'm delighted to hear that. Because if you had done, you'd have been on the next plane straight out of here, all right? Straight back to Macclesfield, all right?

SHARON: Yes, Mr Parks.

VIC: And in the meantime, did you not come equipped with a uniform? Eh?

SHARON: Sorry?

VIC: I said, did you not have a uniform when you arrived here?

36

SHARON: Yes, Mr Parks.

VIC: Then, in future, when you are on duty will you kindly wear it, as you're supposed to do.

SHARON: Yes, Mr Parks.

VIC: Is that understood?

SHARON: Yes, Mr Parks.

VIC: Then get upstairs and get changed. You look disgusting dressed like that, anyway.

(SHARON *rushes off, starting to cry as she goes.* VIC *glares after her.*)

Bloody girl. Do you know how much we're paying for her?

JILL: It's all right, Vic, the kids are fine. Look, they're playing again. They soon forget.

VIC: All right then. Time for a swim. (*Calling to the other end of the pool.*) Look out, you two. Here comes a crocodile . . .

(VIC *goes off to the end of the pool, throwing aside his shirt as he goes. In a second, we hear the diving board vibrate and then a splash as he dives in.*)

JILL: Well, I suppose I'd better go and find my film crew. Wake them up.

DOUGLAS: Well. I'm ready when you are, Jill.

JILL: (*Drily*) Thank you, Mr Beechey. That's most reassuring.

(*She goes out through the garden gate. Throughout the next,* VIC *will occasionally appear at this end of the pool. He is evidently swimming length after length.* DOUGLAS *and* KENNY *watch him idly.* VIC *turns and swims away.*)

KENNY: (*At length*) You know, there's only one thing about that story of Vic's – I mean, it's not the first time I've heard it, naturally – but I've always wondered, why on earth did you do such a bean-brained thing like that? I mean, running straight at a man who's armed with a loaded shotgun? What on earth made you do it?

DOUGLAS: Do you know, I've often asked myself that and I haven't the faintest idea.

KENNY: Do you make a habit of that sort of thing? Sudden reckless gestures? I mean, do you mountaineer, jump out of aeroplanes? Things like that?

DOUGLAS: No. Certainly not.

KENNY: Extraordinary. I don't know about making you a hero.
You were lucky not to have been locked up as a lunatic.
(VIC *appears momentarily at this end of the pool. He turns and
swims back out of view.*)

DOUGLAS: Well, funnily enough, that's exactly what the police
said to me at the time. They called it a very foolhardy,
reckless gesture.

KENNY: They still made a hero of you.

DOUGLAS: I don't think the police did that. That was the press.
They said I'd captured the general public's imagination.

KENNY: No problem. That's about as easy to capture as a dead
chicken in a meat safe. Gallant bank clerk risks life to save
fiancée?

DOUGLAS: So the story went. Actually, Nerys wasn't even my
fiancée. Not at the time.

KENNY: No? I always understood she was.

DOUGLAS: No, she was actually engaged to someone else when it
happened, but – after the – accident – he – her fiancé – broke
it off. And this reporter said it would be an altogether better
story if he could say that Nerys and I were engaged. And I
said it would probably be all right. And he said, well, when
she'd regained consciousness, if subsequently we both went
off the idea and decided to split up again, that would make
another good story.
(VIC *appears briefly again.*)

KENNY: Ah. (*He considers this.*) I see. Well, I think I'll have a dip.
Expose the alabaster limbs. Just go and rout out some
trunks. You're not swimming?

DOUGLAS: No. If it's all the same.

KENNY: It's all the same to me, chum.
(KENNY *saunters into the house. As he does so, he passes*
MARTA, *who comes out of the house and starts, unsmilingly, to
clear the coffee things.*)

DOUGLAS: Very nice cup of coffee. Thank you. *Gracias.* (MARTA
ignores him. DOUGLAS *wanders around and explores the place a
little. The children's shouts are heard, happy again. The distant
splash of water. A plane flies over.* DOUGLAS *shields his eyes
and watches it pass.* VIC *appears once more.*)

38

VIC: (*As he turns, spluttering*) 'S great. You want to try it.
     (*He swims away.* TRUDY *returns from the far end of the pool.*)
TRUDY: (*Calling to the children*) You stay that end. Stay up that
     end, you do hear? Keep an eye on them, won't you, Vic?
     (VIC's *spluttered reply is heard.*)
     (*To* DOUGLAS) Sure you don't want a swim?
DOUGLAS: No, I –
TRUDY: It's lovely and warm . . .
DOUGLAS: No, I – always look a little foolish in the water.
TRUDY: Oh, I'm sure you look fine . . . You should see me. These
     days. I'm no bathing beauty . . .
DOUGLAS: (*Gallantly*) Oh, come now . . .
TRUDY: Nobody'll see you. Not here.
DOUGLAS: It's very peaceful. Quite a contrast. When I left first
     thing this morning it was pouring with rain.
TRUDY: Ah . . .
DOUGLAS: Forty-three degrees.
TRUDY: Yes?
DOUGLAS: Fahrenheit.
TRUDY: Yes.
DOUGLAS: I can never work out the other one, I'm afraid.
TRUDY: No?
DOUGLAS: That's a terrible admission for someone working in
     double glazing.
     (*He laughs.* TRUDY *smiles.* VIC *appears briefly in the pool
     again. They watch him.*)
DOUGLAS: He's a good swimmer, Vic.
TRUDY: Yes, he's very good. Mind you, he can do most things.
     Once he sets his mind to them. I've always said if Vic can't
     do something, then it's probably only because he doesn't
     want to do it in the first place.
     (*She pauses as* SHARON *comes out of the house. She is now
     dressed in her nursemaid's uniform – a little incongruously
     considering the temperature.*)
     Why on earth are you dressed up like that, Sharon? It's
     sweltering.
SHARON: (*Sulkily*) Mr Parks said I had to.
TRUDY: Really? Oh, well. If Mr Parks told you to . . .

39

SHARON: (*Aloof*) Excuse me, please.

(*She marches off towards the pool.* TRUDY *stares at her sourly.*)

DOUGLAS: He certainly tore her off a strip just now, your husband.

TRUDY: Did he?

DOUGLAS: I wouldn't have cared to have been on the receiving end of that.

TRUDY: Don't worry. It always looks worse than it is.

DOUGLAS: Does he do that a lot, then?

TRUDY: Oh, yes. Quite a lot. It's not quite as it appears.

(VIC *appears again briefly.*)

Vic often shouts at women.

DOUGLAS: (*Laughing uncertainly*) I hope not at you.

TRUDY: He's like a lot of men I've met. They don't quite know what to do with a woman when they've got her, so they shout at her.

DOUGLAS: I don't think I've ever shouted at Nerys . . .

TRUDY: No, well, you're probably different. Perhaps you're one of those men who do know what to do with a woman once you've got her . . .

DOUGLAS: (*Laughing self-consciously*) I don't – quite know what to say to that. (*He laughs again.*) I hope I do. (*He laughs.*) I've got a pretty fair idea, yes. (*Pause. Suddenly feeling the heat.*) It's going to be a scorcher, isn't it? A real scorcher.

TRUDY: Would you like to take your jacket off?

DOUGLAS: Er . . .

TRUDY: And your – pullover. You must be very hot.

DOUGLAS: Well, I think, with your permission – the jacket, thank you . . .

(*He removes his jacket.* TRUDY *takes it from him and hangs it on a chair. As this is happening,* VIC *appears again briefly.*)

Thank you.

TRUDY: I'm sorry, I really am.

DOUGLAS: Sorry?

TRUDY: I mean, it must be obvious that I didn't want you to come here – I didn't want to meet you and I didn't want Vic to meet you again. I still don't know why he agreed to it. I suppose Jill must have . . . If you'd brought your wife with

you – I don't know what I'd have done. Probably run away, I
think.

DOUGLAS: There would have been no need for that, I'm sure.

TRUDY: I think you're amazing, I really do. When you think of
what happened to her – and to you – and then you willingly
come here and see us with – all this – Amazing. (*She laughs.*
Pause.) Of course, being only human, it keeps occurring to
me that maybe you want something from us. And maybe you
haven't yet said what it is.

DOUGLAS: Is that how I appear to be?

TRUDY: No, you don't. Not at all. But one can't help wondering,
none the less. Being only human. (*Pause.*) I don't know if
there is anything we can do. I can do. Anything we can give
you. Or offer you. But if there is . . . I mean it. Anything.
Take it. Please. Take it.

(*She looks at* DOUGLAS. *He looks at her.*)

DOUGLAS: (*Gently*) No. Really. There's nothing you have that I
could possibly take. Thank you all the same.

(TRUDY *nods and goes into the house.* DOUGLAS *looks about
him once more. Then sits on a sun lounger.* CINDY, *the child,
runs on from the pool. She is in her swimming costume and her
wet feet leave a trail across the patio. She has a very soggy bunch
of wild grasses and weeds. A child's bouquet. She stands in front
of* DOUGLAS *and holds them out to him.*)
Are these for me?

(CINDY *nods.*)

(*Taking the offering from her*) Thank you very much. How
lovely . . .

(CINDY *rushes away to the pool again.*)

(*As she disappears*) Thank you.

(DOUGLAS *stands holding the bouquet. He looks around him.
Then at the bouquet. The sound of splashing and* VIC *now
playing with the happy children at the other end of the pool.*
DOUGLAS *continues to stand looking around. There is an
expression on his face that could just be the start of a growing
envy.* JILL, *quite suddenly and purposefully, walks out from the
house, into the centre of the patio.*)

JILL: (*Shouting to the invisible film crew*) And cut.

(*The voices from the pool and the splashing stop abruptly.*)
Thank you. Thank you, Douglas.

DOUGLAS: Was that all right?

JILL: Perfect. Thank you. (*To the crew.*) Keep that set up, we've
just got time to do their first meeting before lunch.
(*Shouts from the crew.*)
Yes, we can. We've got nearly fifteen minutes. Douglas, I
want to do yours and Vic's first meeting, all right?

DOUGLAS: (*Putting down his bouquet*) Right-oh, yes.
(JILL *is arranging three of the upright chairs into a loose semi-
circular 'interview' set-up.* DOUGLAS *puts on his jacket again. A
distant call from the crew.*)

JILL: (*In response*) Why not?
(*Distant technical explanation.*)
Well, too bloody bad . . . Dan, I'm replugging now. This
will be a mute sequence. It's just so I can talk to you. All
right?
(*As she fiddles to reconnect her radio mic,* VIC *enters from the
house. He has now changed and is spruced up for TV – a casual,
manly image: blazer, lightweight tropical trousers, sunglasses and
just the right number of shirt buttons undone.*)

VIC: What's going on?

JILL: I just want to do the first meeting with Mr Beechey, Vic – if
you don't mind . . . The one we didn't get earlier.

VIC: Nearly lunchtime, isn't it?

JILL: No, we've got (*consulting her watch*) – twelve and a half
minutes – I literally just want the two of you meeting, OK?
Very simple. All in long. No sound. If I can get the
establishing shot now, then we'll start the interviews after
lunch. Douglas, my love . . .

DOUGLAS: Hallo.

JILL: OK. Listen, I want you simply to come in through that gate
– like this – (*She demonstrates.*) OK?

DOUGLAS: (*Watching her intently*) Yes. I came in the other way,
originally. When I arrived. Does that matter?

JILL: Not in the least.

VIC: This is television. It's all fiction, son. All fiction. (*He winks at*
DOUGLAS.)

42

JILL: (*Slightly coolly*) Not all of it. But in this case it doesn't matter. (*Demonstrating.*) Now, I want you to walk to the middle of the patio – like this – stop – look around you – never seen anywhere like it in your life – gasp, gasp – and then we'll see Vic coming out from the house to greet you. OK?

DOUGLAS: Yes, yes . . .

VIC: You want me from the house?

JILL: Please.

VIC: As soon as he stops?

JILL: Yes. I can talk you through it. It'll be with voice-over this, eventually. I just want you both to meet, apparently start talking for a second or two, and then I'll come out and join you – and we'll sit – here – (*She indicates the three chairs, then into her mic.*) Are you getting all this, Dan? I hope you are, and can you relay it to George? Douglas, can you sit this side – here? (*She indicates one of the side chairs.*)

DOUGLAS: There. Right.

JILL: And Vic, you'll sit here. OK?

VIC: OK.

JILL: Then I can be between you. All right, shall we have a quick run first? Can you both take your places. Douglas, just outside the gate.
(DOUGLAS *hurries back to wait outside the gate, ever co-operative.* VIC *strolls back into the house in a rather more leisurely manner.*)
(*Into her mic*) Dan, will you tell George we'll do it once so he can look at it. OK?
(*She looks in the crew's direction. A shout from them.*)
OK, this is just a rehearsal and – action. Thank you, Douglas. (*She steps back into the house doorway*). Douglas . . . Come on, please . . .
(DOUGLAS *sticks his head round the gate.*)

DOUGLAS: All right?

JILL: Yes, come on. Come on. Keep walking in . . .
(DOUGLAS *walks in through the gate. He has a lot of trouble walking to order. His arms and legs are rather uncoordinated.*)
Come on in further, Douglas. And try not to look at the camera if you can help it . . .

43

DOUGLAS: (*Trying not to move his lips*) Sorry.

JILL: Relax, try and relax, Douglas. Act normally . . .

DOUGLAS: Yes, I'm trying to act normally . . .

JILL: Now, look around you . . . you haven't seen this place before, have you?

DOUGLAS: No.

JILL: Look around then. Take it all in.

DOUGLAS: (*Looking round, still speaking like an unsuccessful ventriloquist*) Yes, I'm taking it in, yes . . .

JILL: Well, look a bit amazed – look a little awed by it all –
(DOUGLAS *tries to look awed.*)
More. More. Isn't it an amazing place, Douglas? You've never seen anything like it in your life . . .
(DOUGLAS *tries to look more awed.*)
Talk if you want to. You can talk if you feel like it . . .

DOUGLAS: (*Looking around*) Sorry. There doesn't seem to be anyone here to talk to –

JILL: (*Muttering, despairingly*) Oh, Jesus . . . Thank you, and cue Vic . . .
(VIC *strides out from the house, hand extended.*)

VIC: (*To* DOUGLAS, *genially*) Hallo . . .

DOUGLAS: (*Equally genial, shaking* VIC's *hand*) Oh, hallo, there.

VIC: Hallo.

DOUGLAS: Hallo.
(*Pause.*)

VIC: (*Laughing*) That's about all I have to say to you.

JILL: Keep talking, please. Just a bit more.

VIC: You must be the man come to deliver the coal?

DOUGLAS: Pardon? (*Getting the joke.*) Oh, yes. Right. I've got it in the van out there.

VIC: Oh, good. You sold your handcart, I take it?

DOUGLAS: Yes, oh, yes. I sold my handcart. Got fifty pesetas for it.
(*He laughs at his own inventiveness.* JILL *emerges from the doorway to join them both.*)

JILL: Yes, OK, something like that. And then I'll say, hallo, sorry to interrupt – this must be quite a strange feeling for you both, meeting after – what is it – seventeen years?

44

DOUGLAS: Yes, seventeen.

VIC: Is it seventeen? Good gracious me.

JILL: And then I'll say something else and then I'll suggest we all
sit down, shall we?
(*She indicates the three chairs.*)

VIC: What a charming idea!

DOUGLAS: Why not? Take the weight off the feet after my long
journey. Phew!

VIC: Good flight was it? Anyone fall out?

DOUGLAS: Wonderful flight. British Airways. You can't beat
them. Not for flying.
(VIC *has sat down in his designated seat.* DOUGLAS, *carried
away by the improvised conversation, has seated himself in the
middle chair.*)

JILL: (*Irritated by all this badinage*) No, Douglas. Douglas . . .

VIC: I think you're meant to be in that one, Mr Coalman.

JILL: This one, please . . . That's mine.

DOUGLAS: Oh, I am sorry. I beg your pardon. Carried away. I
really enjoy filming, you know. I didn't think I would. I
think I could even enjoy it as a career.
(DOUGLAS *sits in his correct seat, as he speaks.* JILL *sits in hers.*)

JILL: OK. Then as soon as we're settled here, I'll cut. And we'll
pick it up after lunch for close-ups in these same positions,
OK?

DOUGLAS: Yes, yes . . . That sounds a good plan.

JILL: All right, Dan? That work all right for George?
(*A distant shout.*)
What?
(*The shout is repeated.*)
Yes, I know, I told him that. (*To* DOUGLAS.) They're saying,
can you try not to notice the camera?

DOUGLAS: Yes, I'm sorry, I'm sorry . . .

VIC: Try and defocus your eyes, that's the tip – otherwise it's very
difficult not to look at it – The camera's like a magnet, you
know what I mean . . .?

DOUGLAS: Yes, yes, thank you . . .

VIC: Defocus . . . That's what I do. That's the way to do it.

DOUGLAS: Thank you very much, I'll try that.

JILL: (*Who has been looking off towards the camera crew*) OK. Here we go for real this time. Places again, please. We're very short of time.

(VIC *goes back into the house.* DOUGLAS *starts for the gate but is called back by* JILL.)

Douglas –

DOUGLAS: Yes, Jill.

JILL: Just – when you meet Vic this time . . . I don't think you want to be – what shall I say – quite so overjoyed to see him . . .

DOUGLAS: Oh, no, no, that was just . . .

JILL: I mean, here's a man you haven't seen for seventeen years and the last time you saw him he was firing a shotgun into the face of the woman you loved – so . . .

DOUGLAS: Yes, I see . . .

JILL: I mean, it just looks odd – if you greet him like a long-lost brother. I think – you know – just a little wariness and a sense that perhaps you haven't *quite* forgiven and forgotten – I mean, I know maybe you have – but it would certainly look more natural – to the average viewer . . . Do you follow?

DOUGLAS: Yes. Yes. No, it was only . . .

(*A yell from the crew.*)

JILL: (*In response to this*) Yes, OK, OK. We have to get on. We've got five minutes. Can you try and give me all that?

DOUGLAS: Yes, I'll try. I'll try.

JILL: Bless you. Thank you, Douglas . . . Thank you very, very deeply.

(DOUGLAS *goes off through the gate.*)

All right, everyone. (*Into her mic.*) Tell George to yell as soon as he's rolling . . . (*A pause.*) Stand by, everyone. One take. That's all we've got.

(*Slight pause. A distant shout.*)

OK. And – action! (*As she retreats right into the house this time.*) Thank you, Douglas.

(*A slight pause.* DOUGLAS *enters through the gate. His eyes are defocused, so he is tending to peer around a little myopically, his eyes screwed up.*)

(*Muttering*) What the hell's he doing, he looks like Mr Magoo

. . . (*Calling.*) That's lovely, Douglas. Keep going. Try and look up a little. Look around the place as you come in . . . Oh, no!

(RUY *has entered by the pool with a hosepipe in his hand. He stops by the edge and watches the proceedings. An ironic cheer from the crew, who are evidently well away.*)

All right. Keep rolling. Keep rolling. Keep going, Douglas. (*Hissing to* RUY.) Back! Back! Piss off!

(RUY *appears not to notice her.*)

(*Into her mic*) Dan! Dan! Can you hear me? Don't let that man wander into shot. Someone get that sodding gardener out of shot. (*Calling.*) Super, Douglas. Perfect. Now, stop there and look around you. Just don't look at the gardener, he's not really there.

(*Someone, unseen, flicks the other end of Ruy's hosepipe to try to attract his attention.* RUY *fails to notice, so engrossed is he in watching* DOUGLAS, *who is staring about him myopically.*)

Come on, Douglas, give us a bit of surprise. (*Hissing angrily into her mic again.*) Will somebody get rid of that bloody gardener . . .

(DOUGLAS *tries to look surprised. Ruy's hosepipe twitches again, rather more violently. He gives it a passing glance but continues to hold on to it, watching intently.*)

Come on, Douglas, real amazement now – (*Furiously into mic.*) Get that half-wit out of shot! All the amazement you can muster now, Douglas.

(DOUGLAS *is staring about him open-mouthed. As he looks at* RUY, *who is standing looking at* DOUGLAS, *equally fascinated, someone gives the hosepipe a really fierce tug.* RUY *is pulled off his feet, overbalances and with a cry falls backwards into the pool.* DOUGLAS *looks genuinely alarmed.*)

DOUGLAS: What happened?

JILL: All right! Ignore that. He'll be OK. Carry on. We're desperately short of time. Cue Vic. Thank you, Vic.

(VIC *comes out of the house, genially, as before.*)

VIC: Hallo . . .

JILL: Remember, suspicious of him, Douglas – suspicious.

DOUGLAS: (*Suspiciously*) Hallo, who are you?

RUY: (*Bobbing up in the swimming pool*) Help!
    (DOUGLAS *turns to see if* RUY *is all right.*)
JILL: Douglas, keep looking at Vic. Remember who he is.
DOUGLAS: Yes, sorry.
VIC: Did you have a good flight?
DOUGLAS: (*Suspiciously*) What do you mean by that exactly?
RUY: (*Coming up again*) Help! Mr Vic!
DOUGLAS: (*Turning again*) Is he all right?
VIC: (*Genially, still*) No, I think he's drowning . . .
JILL: Keep chatting, I need more chat. Don't worry about the
    gardener, he's not in shot. Keep chatting together. Vic,
    point out the garden to Douglas . . .
VIC: (*Obeying her*) Well, now. This is the patio . . .
DOUGLAS: Oh, yes . . .
VIC: You may have noticed it as you walked over it. And that's
    our swimming pool over there . . .
DOUGLAS: Lovely . . .
JILL: Super, that's super, chaps . . .
RUY: (*Coming up again*) Help!
VIC: And that's our gardener over there, coming up for the third
    time . . .
JILL: Keep talking, Douglas. Come on. Time is against us.
DOUGLAS: (*Worried*) Can he swim, do you think?
VIC: I shouldn't imagine so. Not in those boots.
DOUGLAS: Good Lord . . .
RUY: Help! Please! Mr Vic!
    (JILL *moves out to join them as before.*)
JILL: Hallo there, gentlemen, sorry to interrupt –
RUY: Help!
JILL: Vic, Douglas, this must be quite a strange feeling for both
    of you meeting after – what is it – seventeen years?
VIC: Certainly is.
DOUGLAS: I think we ought to do something.
RUY: (*Spluttering*) Aaarrgghh!
DOUGLAS: I really think he's drowning, you know . . .
JILL: Douglas, how does it feel meeting after all this time?
DOUGLAS: (*Distracted by* RUY) What? Oh, very nice, thank you
    very much. (*He smiles.*)

48

JILL: (*Fiercely*) Don't smile. (*Pleasantly again.*) Well, perhaps we should all sit down, should we?

VIC: Good idea.

DOUGLAS: Why not?

RUY: Aaarrgghh!

(*They all go to sit.* DOUGLAS, *distracted, again threatens to sit in the wrong chair.*)

JILL: This chair, Douglas, this one, please.

DOUGLAS: Sorry.

JILL: And chat, chat, chat, chat, chat . . .

VIC: Chat, chat, chat . . .

JILL: (*Getting up again*) And that's it. Super. Thank you both.

RUY: (*Spitting out water*) Ooooorrrggghh!

(JILL *moves towards where the crew are and talks into her mic.*)

JILL: Dan, can you ask George if he managed to keep off that idiot? Did he manage to keep the gardener out of shot . . .? Ask him.

(VIC *moves to* RUY *and starts to pull him, exhausted, from the water.*)

VIC: Come on, you'll be all right. Come on, old lad.

(DOUGLAS *stands watching, amazed.*)

You get off home and have your dinner. You'll feel better then . . . You mustn't interrupt the filming, you know.

RUY: (*Weakly*) No. Thank you, Mr Vic, thank you. Sorry. Sorry.

VIC: There you go . . .

RUY: (*Staggering off along the poolside*) Sorry, Mr Vic . . .

VIC: OK. Don't worry about it, old son.

(RUY *exits gasping and panting. A shout from the crew.*)

JILL: What? He did? Oh, terrific. (*To* VIC *and* DOUGLAS.) That's fine. George apparently managed to pan off the gardener and still keep the full patio in frame, so we're OK. That's great. Lunchtime, is it?

VIC: One minute past one.

JILL: Pretty good going.

VIC: Want a drink first?

(JILL *looks doubtful.*)

Come on, just a little one.

JILL: Well, a little one perhaps . . .

VIC: (*To* DOUGLAS) Doug?

DOUGLAS: Mmm?

VIC: Coming in for lunch?

DOUGLAS: (*Still a little dazed*) Oh, yes. Thank you. Yes.

(*They all move towards the house.* DOUGLAS *stops to pick up his bouquet on the way.*)

JILL: (*As they go*) God, you know, I had this dreadful fear that that man was going to be in shot through the entire sequence. I meant, the thought of having to set the whole thing up again after lunch . . .

(VIC *steps aside to let* JILL, *then* DOUGLAS *enter. Shouts are heard from the crew.*)

VIC: (*Returning to make out what they're saying*) What's that?

(*More shouts.* DOUGLAS *and* JILL *come out again.*)

JILL: What are they saying?

VIC: Apparently you didn't say cut. They just want to know if you'd finished the shot.

JILL: Well, obviously I've finished. Idiots. (*Shouting.*) Of course I've finished. (*Loudly.*) Cut!

(*A sudden blackout.*)

ACT II

Later that same afternoon. At the start, as before, there is just a light on JILL *who sits on the patio doing a piece to camera. The film crew, as always, are out of sight.*

JILL: It became increasingly clear that the quiet, law-abiding, undemanding Douglas Beechey we had met and spoken to in Purley a few days before was a very different creature from the man who had arrived here at the Parks' villa earlier that day. Here was a person who, at last, seemed to have discovered a long-lost purpose. As each of his senses, in turn, took in the unfamiliar – the sweet perfume of luxury, the rich, clean vista of good living, the comfortable, self-confident murmur of opulence – his manner grew ever more watchful – increasingly thoughtful. Were these merely the signs of a man finally coming to terms with his lot? A man at last accepting that most unacceptable of truths – that life *is* unjust? Or was there a darker, more dangerous emotion starting to emerge from this hitherto undemonstrative man. Was this an anger, an envy, even a dim forgotten desire for revenge . . . ? (*She pauses, dramatically.*)
(*As* JILL *has spoken the lights have slowly widened, as before.*)
Cut. (*She rises and talks to the crew.*) That OK?
(*A shouted reply.*)
Yes, thank you very much. I meant technically OK, Dan – I can do without the editorial, thank you. Can we set up in the study now, please? We'll just do Vic's interview, then that's it for today, all right? (*Waving them round.*) Go through the front. Through the front door, it'll be easier. I'll see you there.
(JILL *gathers up her folder from the table. She flicks through it to find her questions for* VIC. KENNY *wanders out with a drink in his hand.*)

KENNY: (*Watching her*) Are you thinking of doing your interview with Vic fairly soon?

JILL: Yes. They're just setting it up . . .

KENNY: You'd better get a move on. The rate he's pouring it down himself, he won't be able to string two words together . . .

JILL: God, I asked him to go easy –

KENNY: Oh, yes? I'll tell him you're nearly ready. In the study?

JILL: I'll be right there. He is forty-seven, isn't he?

KENNY: Forty-seven, yes. Forty-eight next May.

JILL: (*Scribbling this on to her notes*) Does he mind it being mentioned?

KENNY: He never has done.

JILL: If I get Vic done now, then tomorrow morning I can spend with Mr Beechey and that leaves me the rest of the day clear – till our flight, to do general shots of the island . . . Should be all right. Always providing I can get Mr Beechey to say anything remotely interesting . . .

KENNY: He tries his best, I think.

JILL: It was a complete waste of time just now with the three of us. It was all Vic talking. Beechey never said a word –

KENNY: Well, Vic's an expert, isn't he? I mean, he's done hundreds of these things. How many's Douglas done?

JILL: I gave him his chance. Douglas, what do *you* think? Douglas, what do *you* say to that? You heard me. Nothing. Not a usable syllable. (*Excitedly.*) I tell you, Kenny, somehow or other – if I'm going to make any sort of programme – I have got to find a way to prise that man open. Get to the heart of him. I know, you see, I know that under all that suburban – blandness – that dreary flock-wallpaper personality of his – there is a real person there. There is pain – there is disappointment – there is a burning resentment – hopefully even hatred, who knows.

KENNY: Really? Are you sure?

JILL: There has to be. Please God there is.

KENNY: He seems pretty well-balanced to me.

JILL: There has to be. Or the man wouldn't be human.

(DOUGLAS *comes out of the house. He has again removed his jacket.*)

(*Switching her tone with accustomed ease*) Mr Beechey, I was just saying – I want to save you till tomorrow morning. All right? When you're fresh.

DOUGLAS: Just to suit you, Jill. I'll fit in with you. I must say though, after that lunch – not to mention that wine – I think you might be wiser to let me sleep it off. What a host, eh? What a host Vic is. It seems like every day is Christmas Day in this house.

JILL: Don't you drink, normally?

DOUGLAS: Oh, Nerys and I are not averse to the odd glass of mother's ruin. But not quite in this quantity. (*He laughs.*)

KENNY: I'll – er . . . see if Vic's ready.

JILL: Thanks.

(KENNY *goes back into the house.*)

DOUGLAS: So we'll all be flying home tomorrow, eh?

JILL: That's right.

DOUGLAS: Maybe we'll be on the same flight.

JILL: No. I think we're going a little later than you. We've got the odd bit of filming to do tomorrow afternoon.

DOUGLAS: All go, eh?

JILL: Well . . . (*She appears to be considering saying something.*)

DOUGLAS: Then what do you do?

JILL: Er – then we have a look at what we've got – And edit. And then we cut it together using any additional studio sequences we decide to include – using actors – what we call reconstructed action . . .

DOUGLAS: Actors playing us?

JILL: Probably . . .

DOUGLAS: Fascinating. Make sure you get a good-looking one for me, won't you? (*He laughs.*)

JILL: (*Smiling wearily*) And then I link the whole thing together, live, on the day . . .

DOUGLAS: Live. Goodness.

JILL: Well, recorded live. In front of a studio audience, anyway.

DOUGLAS: What about that, then? All that work for just one programme. People just don't realize, do they?

(*A slight pause. When* JILL *speaks, it is in her most simple, honest tone. As of one who really is asking for his help.*)

JILL: Douglas . . . ?

DOUGLAS: Yes?

JILL: May I ask you something? Do you think – do you feel that I've been asking you the right questions?

DOUGLAS: How do you mean?

JILL: Well, let me try and explain. Usually, someone like me, a professional interviewer – well, we try as best we can to get at what we hope is the truth, the core of the person we're interviewing. We ask them what we hope are the right questions and then, hopefully, they respond. Which in turn leads us to ask further questions and slowly we arrive at what we, the interviewer, wants to hear; and, more important, hopefully what you, the interviewee, wants to say. Now, I don't feel in our case that I've really got at the truth of you. Do you see? I haven't – I don't feel I've allowed you, yet, to say what you really, truthfully want to say. Now that is not a fault in you, Douglas. That, I'm ashamed to admit, is a fault in me, the interviewer. And I know, I should be able to cope with that. That's my job. That's what I was trained to do. But in our case, yours and mine, it's just not working. I admit it. And it's very unprofessional of me – but I'm actually appealing to you directly for help.

DOUGLAS: (*Perturbed*) I see. I see. I thought we'd been getting on rather well.

JILL: Douglas, be honest. I have done nothing more than scratch the surface of you. Be honest. Have I?

DOUGLAS: Er . . .

JILL: Some people (*she clicks her fingers*) – you know. No problem. It's all there for the picking – open-cast mining. But I have to say it, in your case, you're a very, very deep shaft indeed, Douglas. Too deep for me.

DOUGLAS: Well, how extraordinary. I've never thought of myself as that . . . You may be right. Maybe you just haven't been asking the correct questions.

JILL: Take you and Nerys, for instance.

DOUGLAS: Yes?

JILL: I mean, you've never really talked about your relationship with her. Are you happy together, for instance?

DOUGLAS: Yes.

JILL: Truly happy?

DOUGLAS: Yes.

JILL: No problems?

54

DOUGLAS: No. Not really. I can't think of any, offhand.

JILL: Despite the fact that she can't face leaving the house?

DOUGLAS: Well, that's true, yes. But we've both learnt to live with that, you see . . .

JILL: Doesn't it upset her?

DOUGLAS: No. She doesn't seem to mind. She doesn't want to go anywhere.

JILL: Doesn't she get lonely?

DOUGLAS: No. She's never said so.

JILL: What, all alone in that little house? Every day, while you're out at work?

DOUGLAS: She isn't all alone. People come to visit her.

JILL: Who do?

DOUGLAS: Friends, relations . . .

JILL: She has friends?

DOUGLAS: Dozens of them. They're always dropping in to see her. There's two of them staying there now.

JILL: Women?

DOUGLAS: Yes, of course, women . . . And possibly her uncle Reg, if he can take the day off from the pet shop.

JILL: But surely, Douglas . . . Douglas, there must be more in life for you both than just sitting together day after day in that damp little house . . . ?

DOUGLAS: No, it's not damp. That's one of the good things about it . . .

JILL: But coming here – seeing all this – the pool, the villa, the sunshine . . . Wouldn't you like this for Nerys, at least? Even if not for yourself? Doesn't she deserve it after what she went through? Wouldn't you both adore to have all this, in your heart of hearts?

DOUGLAS: Frankly, no, I'm sorry, we wouldn't. Neither of us swims, Nerys is allergic to sunlight and, personally, I can't get on with Spanish food, not at all.

JILL: (*Growing desperate*) Well, somewhere else. Italy?

DOUGLAS: No.

JILL: Greece? Sweden?

DOUGLAS: No, no. Not attracted, sorry. Despite their standard of living, they always look a rather glum sort of people, don't you think? They certainly do on the television.

JILL: Well, you can't always go by everything – (*She checks herself.*) Possibly.

DOUGLAS: You know, I have to say this, you're making me feel rather guilty, Jill. I'm sorry if I'm being a disappointment. I'd have thought, though, that with all that misery you seem to meet up with in your job every day, a happy, contented couple might make a nice change for once. Wouldn't you have thought?

JILL: (*In exasperation*) Sorry, Douglas, no. They wouldn't. Not at all. Happy, contented couples – happy, contented, middle-aged couples especially – do not make exciting films, they do not make watchable plays or readable books. Nobody wants to hear about them. Nobody's interested in them. Nobody even wants to look at paintings of them. And they certainly don't want to sit down and watch them on television. Happy, contented people are box-office death, Douglas. Because they generally come over as excruciatingly boring. They come over as smug and self-satisfied and superior and they drive the rest of us up the bloody wall and we really don't want to know about them. Not at all. All right?

(*A pause.* DOUGLAS *considers this calmly, seemingly unoffended.*)

DOUGLAS: (*Quietly*) How sad. That's all I can say. How very sad.

JILL: (*Realizing that she has been very rude, even by her standards*) I'm sorry.

DOUGLAS: No . . .

JILL: If you and Nerys really are that rare and precious thing, a blissfully happy married couple, who am I to come between you . . . ? (*Gathering up her things.*) Well, I must see how my crew are getting on . . .

DOUGLAS: Good luck.

(JILL *goes to leave but turns back again, just before she does so.*)

JILL: (*Incredulously*) No, I'm sorry, I can't believe it. You are both *completely* happy?

DOUGLAS: (*Worriedly*) Yes, I think we are. I was trying to think . . .

JILL: Excuse me, but – sexually, as well?

56

DOUGLAS: (*Blankly*) Sexually?

JILL: Sexually, you know. Sex? Long winter evenings? And so on?

DOUGLAS: Well, no, we don't – No.

JILL: You don't?

DOUGLAS: No.

JILL: You mean you don't sleep together?

DOUGLAS: Yes, we sleep together, we just don't – No .

JILL: Ever?

DOUGLAS: No. Not for some little while.

JILL: What do you mean by some little while?

DOUGLAS: Er – probably about fifteen years, probably.

JILL: (*Stunned*) Fifteen years.

DOUGLAS: Yes, I should think – I should think about that, yes.

JILL: (*Appalled*) My God, how have you both managed . . . ?

DOUGLAS: Oh, I don't think it's ever been a problem –

JILL: Fifteen years? I don't believe it. *Fifteen years*? (*Pause.*) You're joking. Fifteen *years*? Did you never try to talk to anyone about it?

DOUGLAS: No, we never felt the need. Anyway, I didn't think anyone would be very interested. We – you know – we tried it for a couple of years when we first got married and– neither of us – found much to it, really – rather over-rated, really – so we gave it up . . .

JILL: Sorry. I have to sit down. (*She does so.*)

DOUGLAS: You all right?

JILL: (*Laughing weakly*) Yes. I couldn't include this in a programme, they wouldn't believe it . . .

DOUGLAS: Oh, I don't know. It's not that uncommon, you know. Nerys's Uncle Reg told me he'd never tried it at all and he's never missed it . . .

JILL: Maybe it's genetic. (*Slight pause.*) *Fifteen years*? And you have never had it? Do you realize, Douglas, there are some of us, many of us, most of us, who spend all our waking hours thinking about having it and at night, if we're not having it, we dream about having it? We spend most of our lives trying to work out how we can get someone to have it with us and then, once we've had it, how we can get rid of the person

57

we're having it with, so we can have it with somebody else? And you've never even bothered to have it . . . I don't believe it. And Nerys feels the same? She doesn't miss it either?

DOUGLAS: She's never said she has.

JILL: What about children? Did she never want children?

DOUGLAS: (*Quickly*) No. Never. She –

JILL: What?

DOUGLAS: She never did. (*Pause.*) I think that maybe as a result of – her accident . . . she felt unable to cope with the responsibility of children.

JILL: And you?

DOUGLAS: Oh, I quite understood why. I appreciated her decision.

JILL: But would you have liked children, if she'd been willing?

DOUGLAS: Possibly.

JILL: You'd have liked them? In other circumstances?

DOUGLAS: (*Cautiously*) Yes . . .

JILL: If, for instance, she hadn't been injured, you'd both probably have had them?

DOUGLAS: (*Uncomfortably*) Er – who can say? Possibly.

JILL: (*Seeing some light at last*) Yes. Right. (*Moving into the house once more, briskly.*) We might talk further about children tomorrow, Douglas. In our interview. All right?

DOUGLAS: (*Unhappily*) Yes. Yes, if you like.

(JILL *goes into the house. She seems rather triumphant.*
DOUGLAS *wanders out towards the pool. He is thoughtful. It is mid-afternoon and very hot.* RUY *comes through the garden gate with a block of rough stone, one of several such journeys he will make during the next.*)

DOUGLAS: Hallo.

(RUY, *as always, doesn't even acknowledge* DOUGLAS's *presence.*)

Dried off, I hope? (*He laughs.*)

(*A bird sings. A plane drones overhead.* DOUGLAS *looks up again.* VIC *comes out on to the terrace, followed by* KENNY. VIC *has apparently had a bit to drink.*)

KENNY: She says they're nearly ready.

VIC: Well, they know where I am if they want me, don't they? It's too hot to sit in there.

(*He sits in the shade.* KENNY *does likewise.*)

(*Calling to* DOUGLAS) Get sunstroke if you stand around out there too long, mate.

DOUGLAS: (*Turning*) Pardon?

VIC: I said, be careful in the sun. If you're not used to it.

DOUGLAS: Oh, yes. Thank you. ((*Returns to the terrace and sits with them.*) I thought you'd be doing your interview.

KENNY: They're not quite ready.

DOUGLAS: Oh.

(*Pause.*)

Do you think ours went all right? Our interview?

VIC: (*Without enthusiasm*) It was all right.

DOUGLAS: You were wonderful. Never stuck for an answer.

VIC: Well . . .

KENNY: He's done it before. Once or twice.

DOUGLAS: Yes, I'm afraid that showed, so far as I was concerned. I'm afraid she floored me once or twice. I was completely speechless. She said she'd be able to cut them out, though. My hesitations. Ah.

(MARTA *has come from the house with a freshly opened bottle of wine and some glasses on a tray. She places them beside* VIC. *During the next,* RUY *returns empty-handed from the swimming pool and goes out through the gate.*)

MARTA: Mr Vic . . .

VIC: Thank you, Marta. Is my wife coming out here, then?

MARTA: Mrs Parks is doing washing up, Mr Vic.

VIC: Why is she doing the washing up?

MARTA: I don't know, Mr Vic . . .

VIC: You should be doing the bloody washing up, not her. That's what you're paid for.

MARTA: I don't know, Mr Vic . . .

VIC: You do the washing up, all right? Tell her to come out here.

MARTA: (*Going back inside*) Yes, Mr Vic . . .

(VIC *pours himself a glass of wine.*)

VIC: I don't know . . . (*Holding up the bottle rather belatedly.*) Anybody?

59

DOUGLAS: No, thank you.

KENNY: (*Gently*) Go steady, Vic.

VIC: (*Mimicking*) Go steady. You sound like my auntie, you great fruit . . . (*He drinks.*) No, I'll tell you something about interviews and being interviewed. The first thing you've got to remember is that, generally speaking, if you are the one being interviewed and feeling nervous, then the person interviewing you – nine times out of ten – he's even more nervous than you are. Because if it all goes wrong, if you cock the whole thing up, all you stand to do is make a fool of yourself – whereas for him – well, it's his job on the line, isn't it? Know what I mean?

(RUY *returns through the gate with another piece of stone. He exits round the swimming pool.*)

DOUGLAS: Yes, I see. That hadn't occurred to me, I must say.

KENNY: (*Who has been watching* RUY) What's he doing there?

VIC: Ruy? He's building a bench – a little stone seat, the other end of the swimming pool . . .

DOUGLAS: Clever.

VIC: Well, he's really a stone mason. But he's had a spot of bother with the local law . . . No, the other thing you've got to remember about an interview is that, normally, whoever's interviewing you will know less about what you're talking about than you do. Because nine times out of ten, he'll be talking to you about you – which makes you the resident expert, doesn't it? As far as you're concerned, it's a home game. He'll be nervous just coming down the tunnel, even before he's started. You see, there's an art to being interviewed. First, you've got to be able to use an interview to your own advantage. I mean, after all, what is an interview? This guy is more often than not trying to get you to say one thing – usually incriminating. And you, on the other hand, are wanting to say something of your own, entirely different to what he wants you to say. So it's a battle to the death, isn't it? If you're being interviewed, you have to turn it around, see? You say things like – that's a very good question, John, and I'd like to answer it if I may – with a question of my own. That always throws them, because they can't bear getting questions back at them. Because they're not usually geared for answers. Only for questions. Because they're interviewers, see, and not meant to have opinions. So they can't answer, anyway. But when they don't, that makes them look furtive. And when he does get a question in, if you don't like the one he's asked you, then give him an answer to another one . . . And when he interrupts you – which he will do, once he realizes that you're giving him the wrong answer, you say to him, I really must be allowed to answer this question in my own way, John, please. And look a bit hurt whilst you're saying it. 'Cause that'll make him look a pushy bastard, too. And another tip, if you're giving an answer and you do happen to know the answer and don't mind giving it to him, talk as fast as you can while still making sense, but don't whatever you do leave pauses. Because they're looking for pauses, see, to edit you about and change your meaning. That's when they put in those nodding bits, you've seen them, when the bloke's nodding his head for dear life about bugger all and sitting in a different room. But if you don't pause, they can't get in to edit, can they? And if they can't edit you, they've either got to leave the interview out altogether, which means they haven't got a programme, which is generally disaster time, or they have to put in what you said in its entirety and not some version of what some monkey would have liked you to have said if he'd got the chance to edit you. And if you're in full flow and you do run out and you do have to stop, stop suddenly. Just like that. (*Quick pause.*) OK? Because that throws him as well. Because nine out of ten, if it's a long answer you've been giving him, he won't be listening, anyway. He'll either be looking at his notes or at the floor manager, or wondering, how long's this bleeder going on for? And if none of that works and you're really up against it, have a choking fit, throw yourself on the floor, knock the mic over and call for water. That usually does the trick.

(*A pause.* DOUGLAS *digests this.*)

DOUGLAS: There's a lot more to it than you imagine, isn't there?
KENNY: True, very true.

(RUY *crosses back to the garden gate, empty-handed again. They watch him.* VIC *pours himself another glass of wine.* SHARON *comes out of the house and walks through the men. She is still in her uniform and is evidently very hot. Her face is lobster-coloured and she is moving slowly and heavily. She ignores them as she passes through and heads towards the swimming pool. But there is something self-conscious in her walk that tells us she is aware of their eyes on her. She stoops to pick up one of the children's toys.*)

DOUGLAS: (*As she does this*) Yes, but I think for the layman, such as myself, it's probably better just to answer the –

VIC: (*Watching* SHARON) Dear, oh dear, oh dear . . .

DOUGLAS: Pardon?

VIC: Just look at the ass on that girl . . .

KENNY: (*Less enthusiastically*) Yes.

VIC: Look at it. Acres of it, isn't there?

(SHARON *goes off round the side of the swimming pool.*)
(*Watching her go*) Dear, oh dear . . . (*To* DOUGLAS , *who has been rather embarrassed.*) Sorry, Doug, you were saying . . . Sorry, I interrupted you.

DOUGLAS: (*Who has forgotten what he was saying*) No, I was – No, I was just saying, put like you were putting it, it all seems a bit like a game, doesn't it?

VIC: What?

DOUGLAS: Interviews. On television.

VIC: Well, they are. Most of them. That shock you, does it?

DOUGLAS: No. Only occasionally, you know, people might genuinely be trying to say something, mightn't they? That they felt deeply about?

(KENNY *laughs drily.* RUY *returns with another block of stone.*)
I wouldn't like to think it was all just nothing more than a game.

VIC: (*Pouring himself another glass of wine*) We all play games, don't we? One way or the other? We all do it.

DOUGLAS: Do you think so?

VIC: Like – right now – I'm wondering what yours might be . . .

DOUGLAS: (*Startled*) What?

VIC: No, seriously. I'm very, very curious. What are you after, sunshine? Smiling away there. What are you after?

KENNY: Vic . . .

VIC: Well, don't tell me he came out here just to tell me what a nice man I am. What a lovely place I've got. Don't tell me he came all this way for that, because, frankly, I don't believe him.

KENNY: He came to do the programme, Vic . . .

VIC: Don't kid me. The programme? You mean to tell me he did all this for a programme? Just so he could see himself on the telly? I don't believe it . . .

DOUGLAS: I'm sorry, but I did . . .

VIC: Well, I'm sorry, but I don't believe you.

DOUGLAS: I did. (*Slight pause.*) Well, and to – (*He checks himself.*)

VIC: What? And to what?

DOUGLAS: And to – see you.

VIC: To see me?

DOUGLAS: Yes.

VIC: I shouldn't have thought you'd have wanted to see me again, would you?

DOUGLAS: Well, when Jill first wrote to us, I must say I didn't, no. But in the end – after Nerys and I had both talked about it – we decided I had to, really.

VIC: Why?

DOUGLAS: You – you're . . . This might sound peculiar, but . . . Because you're still there. In our dreams, you see. After seventeen years. We still both dream about you. We wake up occasionally. In the night. Nerys has this terrible fear – it's quite ridiculous, I've told her – that one night you're going to break in downstairs and come up to get her. I've said to her, it's ridiculous – I mean, there you are on the telly twice a week or something, helping the kids or telling the old folk to mind how they go – I said, he's not going to want to break in here, Nerys – Not after seventeen years, is he? Still. You can't always control your imagination, can you? No matter how hard you try. So, don't take this wrong, but I was hoping this – meeting – might help to exorcize you. If you follow me. I told you it would sound peculiar.

(*A silence.* KENNY *looks at* VIC *a little apprehensively. Suddenly* VIC *laughs. He laughs loud and long. The wine helps.* RUY *returns during this and goes out through the garden gate.*)

VIC: Well, I . . . (*He wipes his eyes.*) Well, I've been called a . . .
I've been called a lot of things . . . (*Controlling himself a little.*)
Look. Listen, Doug. I promise. I promise – you tell Nerys –
tell her I'll never break in through her front window, all
right? Tell her she's perfectly safe. I mean, I've been called a
lot of things. (*To* KENNY) That's wonderful. Isn't that
wonderful?

(SHARON *returns from the swimming pool. Walking slowly, as
before, she carries an armful of the children's toys.*)

Hey, Sharon . . .

SHARON: (*Stopping*) Yes, Mr Parks?

VIC: Where're Timmy and Cindy?

SHARON: They're having their tea in the kitchen with Marta, Mr
Parks.

VIC: Sit down, then.

SHARON: I've got to go and –

VIC: Sit down.

SHARON: Yes, Mr Parks.

(SHARON *sits, still holding on to the toys. She is obviously hotter
than ever and slightly breathless.*)

VIC: Get your breath back.

SHARON: Thank you . . .

VIC: Look at her. Puffing like a grampus, aren't you?

SHARON: Yes, Mr Parks.

VIC: Sweat running off you. (*To the others.*) Look at her. Have you
ever seen anyone sweating like that? It's dripping off her. I
bet it's running off you underneath there, isn't it, eh? Eh?

(SHARON *doesn't reply.*)

Running down your arms? Trickling down your legs? If
there's one thing I hate, it's to see a woman sweating like
that. It's bad enough on a man, it's obscene on a woman,
don't you agree?

(SHARON *sits unhappily.* RUY *crosses with another block of
stone.*)

I'll tell you something, Sharon. Do you know why you're
sitting there, sweating like that? Do you know the reason
why you're sat there like a great bowl of pork dripping? Do

you want to know the reason? Because you are overweight, girl. You are fat. Let's face it, Sharon, you are a fat girl, aren't you? A big, fat girl.

DOUGLAS: Oh, I don't think that's fair, she's just . . .

VIC: Here, let her tell you something, just a second. Sharon . . .

SHARON: Yes, Mr Parks . . .

VIC: Shall we tell them why you're so fat? Shall we? Shall we tell them your secret? It's because you are greedy, isn't it, Sharon? You eat too much. You are a guts. Aren't you? You're a glutton. Eh?

SHARON: Yes, Mr Parks.

VIC: Tell them what you ate on your last birthday, Sharon. Tell them. This girl, she told me that last year on her birthday, she sat on her own, in her flat in wherever it was – Macclesfield –

SHARON: Huddersfield . . .

VIC: Huddersfield. She sat there all on her own, singing happy birthday to me and she ate . . . What did you eat, Sharon? Tell them what you ate, go on.

SHARON: (*Muttering*) Twelve rum babas.

VIC: Come on, say it louder . . .

SHARON: (*Loudly*) Twelve rum babas, Mr Parks.

VIC: Twelve rum babas. Can you imagine that? Turns you over, doesn't it? Still, we're working on you, aren't we, Sharon? We're slowly melting you down, aren't we?

SHARON: Yes, Mr Parks . . .

VIC: Getting her fit. Giving her some exercise. Working it off her. What were you learning this morning then? What was I teaching you this morning, Sharon?

SHARON: Scuba diving, Mr Parks.

VIC: Scuba diving. She enjoyed that – didn't you?

SHARON: Yes.

VIC: You should have seen her in her big black rubber suit flailing about in the water there, first thing. Like a big shiny, beached, humpbacked whale, weren't you . . .
(SHARON *suddenly starts to cry very quietly*.)

DOUGLAS: Look, I'm sorry, this is very, very cruel and unnecessary and I really don't think you should go on

65

tormenting this girl simply because –

VIC: You mind your own business –

DOUGLAS: (*Undaunted*) – simply because she's a shade overweight and obviously very self-conscious about it, anyway. It is cruel and it is hurtful and it is –

VIC: (*Suddenly yelling at him*) I said, mind your own bloody business!

(*A silence.* SHARON *gets up and runs into the house. She passes* TRUDY *who is coming out.* TRUDY *looks at the men and appears to sum up the scene.* RUY *crosses again, empty-handed.*)

(*To* DOUGLAS, *softly*) I hope I don't have to remind you again that you are a guest in this house. And the way I choose to treat my staff is entirely my concern. OK?

(DOUGLAS *is silent.* KENNY *clears his throat.*)

KENNY: They should be about set up for that interview, I should think . . .

TRUDY: They were nearly ready, yes.

VIC: I've been waiting here. Patiently. Plenty of things I could have been getting on with, too.

TRUDY: (*Brightly*) I wondered if you wanted to take up my offer and stroll down to the beach, Douglas? While they're doing their interview?

DOUGLAS: Oh, lovely, yes. Thank you very much.

VIC: (*Sourly*) Yes, you take him down the beach, good idea.

TRUDY: (*Faintly sarcastic*) Oh, dear. You haven't been disagreeing with my husband, have you? I hope not.

DOUGLAS: No, I –

TRUDY: You mustn't do that, you know. He only likes people who agree with him all the time. It's one of his little whims.

VIC: What are you talking about?

TRUDY: It comes of being surrounded by people who nod at him all day at work. He prefers us all to nod at home, too . . .

VIC: (*Innocently*) What did I do, eh? What am I meant to have done, now?

KENNY: (*Laughing*) Can't imagine.

TRUDY: He surrounds himself with these little nodding animals. It's like the back shelf of a car in our house. We all do it.

VIC: Bloody rubbish.

TRUDY: Yes, quite right, dear. Nod, nod.

VIC: What a load of rubbish. (*To* KENNY.) Isn't it? A load of rubbish?

KENNY: (*Nodding*) Oh, yes.

TRUDY: (*To* DOUGLAS) It's about a mile's walk down there. Do you mind?

DOUGLAS: No, I'd like a walk.

VIC: Take the jeep.

TRUDY: No, we want a walk.

VIC: Be quicker in the jeep . . .

TRUDY: No, we want to walk. It's healthier . . .

VIC: Healthier? What are you talking about, healthier?

TRUDY: Healthier. Walking.

VIC: All right then, walk if you want to walk. I think everyone around here is just trying to wind me up, for some reason . . .
(RUY *has entered with another block of stone.*)
(*Yelling jovially*) That's it, Ruy, lad. Get stuck in there, boy . . .

RUY: (*Beaming, despite the exertion*) Yes, Mr Vic. You bet.
(RUY *goes out.*)

TRUDY: What's he building now? Not another garden seat?

VIC: Why not?

TRUDY: Because he keeps building them and then you tell him to pull them down again . . .

VIC: Because they were in wrong place, that's why.

TRUDY: Well, I hope this one's in the right place.

VIC: I'll tell you that when he's built it.
(JILL *comes out from the house.*)

JILL: Vic, Kenny – I'm most dreadfully sorry to have kept you waiting. Believe it or not, we are now finally ready to go when you are.

VIC: Hooray –

JILL: First, we had glare from the window, so we moved round and then we couldn't get back far enough for the two shot . . .

VIC: (*Rising, impatiently*) Come on. Let's get it over with . . .
(VIC *goes inside, taking his glass with him. He passes* MARTA, *who comes out to clear the tray and remaining glasses.*)

JILL: Kenny, you'll want to sit in, of course . . .

KENNY: Well, I'd better. Just in case he says something your lawyers will regret later –

JILL: (*Laughing*) Oh, hardly. Surely not.

KENNY: He's been known to. On occasions . . .

(KENNY *goes into the house.* JILL *is about to follow but lingers to watch* TRUDY *and* DOUGLAS. TRUDY *has moved off the patio to look at what* RUY *is building.* DOUGLAS *has moved to join her.* MARTA, *in due course, follows* KENNY *into the house.*)

TRUDY: (*Turning to* DOUGLAS, *smiling*) Well, shall we go?

DOUGLAS: (*Smiling back*) Ready when you are.

(TRUDY *and* DOUGLAS *go out through the gate.* JILL *watches them go . The lights close down on to her, like a smooth, zooming close up.*)

JILL: (*Solemnly, to camera*) After seventeen long years, the strands were finally being drawn together – individual threads in a tapestry shaped over the years by the hands of countless separate participants – none of whom perhaps, individually, was consciously aware of the final picture which was slowly and inevitably being woven around them. And that picture? No less a portrait than the face of human tragedy . . . (*She pauses.*) (*Calling*) I may need to do that bit again later, George . . . (*Yelling back to them as she goes inside.*) Sorry. Cut!

(*The lights change abruptly on her shout. It is suddenly a moonlit evening. Patches of shadow. Cicadas chirping. Very romantic. Perhaps marred slightly by some very syrupy country and western music emanating distantly from the hi-fi somewhere in the house. Pause.*

In a moment, TRUDY *and* DOUGLAS *come through the gate. They have evidently just returned from their walk.*)

DOUGLAS: I'm afraid we've taken rather longer than we should have done.

TRUDY: No, we've only been a couple of hours. It gets dark much quicker out here. You get used to it after a bit. (*Looking towards the house.*) It doesn't sound as if anyone's missed us particularly, does it?

DOUGLAS: They can't still be filming, surely?

TRUDY: (*Looking back through the gate*) The crew must have gone

back to the hotel. Their van's gone, anyway. And her hire
car. She's gone too. Thank God.

DOUGLAS: Ah, well. My turn tomorrow. In the hot seat.

TRUDY: Are you looking forward to it?

DOUGLAS: (*Uncertain*) Well . . .

TRUDY: I wouldn't be, I must say.

DOUGLAS: I think the problem is that – well, what Jill would
really like is a bit of conflict. She was saying to me at lunch
that a good programme has got to have a bit of conflict. It
needs conflict, otherwise people tend to switch off,
apparently. Mind you, I don't. There's nothing I like better
than a programme with no conflict in it at all. Nerys is the
same. But obviously we're in a minority there. Everyone else
seems to prefer to see people beating each other's brains out.
Extraordinary. So, to create a bit of conflict, I think Jill
would really like me to say a lot of things I don't particularly
care to say. That's the trouble.

TRUDY: Like what?

(DOUGLAS *makes to move on towards the house.*)
(*Stopping him*) No, stay here a minute . . . Like what? What
does she want you to say?

DOUGLAS: Oh . . .

TRUDY: No, you must tell me. I need to know. We must talk, you
see. Mustn't we? It's been a lovely walk but we haven't really
talked, have we? And we need to. We do, you know. And it
has to be you and me. You can never talk to Vic, not about
something he doesn't want to talk about, anyway. Nobody
can. I mean, I'd have talked to your wife if she'd been here.
But she isn't. And she obviously doesn't want to meet us or
have anything to do with us, which is perfectly
understandable. So it has to be us two, you see. Doesn't it?
(*Pause.*) I mean, I need to know how you feel. How you
really feel. You're very good at covering up, but . . . (*Pause.*)
Do you see why I need to know? You must see. I have to
know if you've forgiven us, you understand?

DOUGLAS: Us?

TRUDY: Yes. I'm a part of Vic. I married him, knowing what he'd
done to another human being. To another woman. And I had

his children knowing that. I took on all of him. What do they say these days? (*Smiling faintly*.) A wife should be responsible for her husband's debts. (*Pause*.) So. I need to know.

DOUGLAS: I think, quite honestly, what's past is past, isn't it?

TRUDY: You really don't bear any resentment for what he did? To you? To your wife? The woman you were in love with? Didn't it matter? It's like it never mattered to you at all.

DOUGLAS: Oh, it mattered. Then. Of course it did. Only – Well, it wasn't as straightforward as that. It never is. Let me try and – explain, then. It's difficult. (*Pause*.) Working with me in this bank – I was twenty-four – twenty-five at the time – working with me, alongside me – was the most beautiful woman I have ever seen in my life, anywhere. Before or since. Her name was Nerys Mills and she was a stunner. And I was – besotted. That's the only word for it. Some days I couldn't look at her at all. My hands would shake and my voice used to crack and go falsetto when I spoke and I'd feel sick in my stomach, and one day I actually started crying without any warning at all. Right in the middle of serving a customer. In the end, I had to pretend I got hay fever. And that was very inconvenient, because then I had to remember to keep having it and take nose drops and things, otherwise people would begin to wonder what was really wrong with me. Anyway, needless to say – Nerys didn't take a blind bit of notice of me. No, that's not exactly true. She was generally very nice and polite, but, so far as romance went, I think I was definitely at the bottom of the reserves as far as she was concerned. She was actually unofficially engaged to this other man – (*Darkly*.) I forget his name now. I never forget names but I've forgotten his.

TRUDY: Did he work in the bank as well?

DOUGLAS: No, no. He was a salesman. A double-glazing salesman, actually. There's an amusing story to that, I'll come back to that. Anyway, I sat there and – longed for her – day after day – month after month – fantasized about her a little – nothing unpleasant, you know . . .

TRUDY: No, no . . .

DOUGLAS: And some mornings she'd have a chat with me

between customers. And then the sun would shine all day, you know . . . (*He smiles.*)

TRUDY: (*Smiling*) Yes . . .

DOUGLAS: And other mornings, she'd come in like thunder – something obviously had gone wrong the night before with her and old double-glazing . . . And then, of course, you never got a smile . . .

TRUDY: (*Sadly*) Ah . . .

DOUGLAS: And as time went by, I marked her off in my own personal ledger in the desirable but unattainable column, along with the Silver Cloud and the offer to keep wicket for Kent – and I was just resigning myself to life without her and seriously considering whether the Royal Army Pay Corps might have a vacancy somewhere – when the bank raid occurred. And that did change everything. There's no doubt about it. I don't know why I did what I did. Your husband was right, it was madness. It just seemed the only thing to do at the time, that's all. There was this stranger in a balaclava threatening the woman that I cared more than my own life for . . . I couldn't help myself, you see?

TRUDY: (*Engrossed*) No. I see. I see.

DOUGLAS: Afterwards, I went to see her a lot in hospital. Partly through guilt. Only partly. But, you see, if I hadn't run at Vic like that, she might never have – Not that she's ever blamed me. She's never once, ever – Never. Anyway, I went to see her, as soon as they'd let us in to visit. I imagined there's be so many blokes round the bed she'd never even see me, anyway. And there were, to start with. I was just there waving my bunch of daffodils at her from the back of the crowd. And then slowly they all drifted away. Over the weeks. Stopped coming to see her.

TRUDY: How rotten. Aren't people rotten, sometimes?

DOUGLAS: Yes, I thought that at first. Then I realized later, of course. She'd been sending them all away. Subconsciously. A beautiful woman like she'd been, she couldn't bear to be seen like – that. She couldn't stand it. I mean, she wasn't vain. Not really. But if you're used all your life to people taking pleasure in looking at you, then it must be very hurtful when they suddenly start instinctively looking away from you. You couldn't blame people, altogether. She did look a terrible mess for a time.

TRUDY: But you didn't? Look away from her?

DOUGLAS: Well, I think I probably did, yes. As I say, it was only natural early on. But, you see, if I looked away from her, it didn't matter quite so much. Because she'd never valued my opinion of her anyway. So it never worried her. And there I was, with her all to myself. Visiting every day. Jollying her up. And over the weeks we got very friendly.

TRUDY: And did she fall in love with you?

DOUGLAS: I don't know.

TRUDY: But did she never say to you . . . ?

DOUGLAS: No. And I didn't ask her. It didn't matter. She liked me. And more important, she needed me. That's what mattered. And I loved her. (*He smiles.*) I was going to tell you, you know, when I'd left the bank, I applied for my present job with this double-glazing company. I thought it might – you know – increase my standing with her. Since she seemed to have a liking for double-glazing men. Ridiculous. We laughed about that later. I never regretted it, though. They're a grand bunch. Anyway, she came out. And we married quietly. And we got a joint mortgage on number fifty-three and we've lived there ever since. With never a cross word, I'm happy to report. (*Pause.*) So what do I say? Yes, I do – I hate Vic because of what he did to the most beautiful woman in the world? Or, thank you very much, Vic, for being instrumental in arranging for me to marry the unattainable girl of my dreams? Difficult to know which to say, isn't it? (*Pause.*) All right. I know you might well say, what about her? What about poor old Nerys? Being forced to settle for minor league when she was naturally first division. Well, all I can say is, without prejudice, and I am not a swearing person, you appreciate – but that man she was engaged to originally – old double-glazing the first – he was a complete – pillock. He really was. He treated Nerys like – well, there were times when – not just me, you understand . . . We all could have done – in that bank. Including Mr

Marsh. This man – he treated her as only a handsome man
can treat a beautiful woman. If you know what I mean.

TRUDY: Yes. I do. I think I do.

(*They listen to the music for a moment.*)

DOUGLAS: (*Cheerfully*) Well, that's – that's my life. Sorry if I
bored you. (*Pause.*) This is very pleasant music, isn't it?
Country and western? Am I right?

TRUDY: (*Weakly*) Yes. Vic likes it. We used to . . . When we were
. . . (*Her voice tails away.*)

(DOUGLAS *waits for her to finish the sentence. She doesn't. She
is evidently in some distress. She rocks about. She looks at*
DOUGLAS. *Suddenly and unexpectedly, she kisses him on the
mouth. Then pulls away and avoids his look. He, after taking a
second to recover, avoids her in turn. They sit, pretending it
hasn't happened.*)

DOUGLAS: (*At length*) Yes, I'm very partial to country and
western music. They always manage to come up with a good
tune, don't they?

TRUDY: (*In a little voice*) I'm sorry. (*Then, pulling herself together.*)
There's nothing we can do for you, then? Vic and I?
Nothing?

DOUGLAS: Do?

TRUDY: Well, to help in any way . . . Money or . . .

DOUGLAS: (*Rather embarrassed*) Oh, no.

TRUDY: (*Equally embarrassed*) Sorry. I didn't mean to –

DOUGLAS: No, no . . .

TRUDY: It's just so rare to meet someone who doesn't want
something from us these days . . . I suppose that's called
being successful. Or is it because it's us who are offering? Is
that why you're saying you don't want anything?

DOUGLAS: No, it's not that. I just don't think there is anything.
Thank you very much. Well, I think I must away down the
hill to my own hotel. They'll be serving dinner soon . . .

TRUDY: You're welcome to stop and have supper with us if you –

DOUGLAS: No, that's very kind of you, but you'll see quite
enough of me again tomorrow.

TRUDY: Well, wait there a second, I'll fetch the keys and run you
back –

73

DOUGLAS: No, please.

TRUDY: It's no trouble –

DOUGLAS: I'd rather walk, I really would. Really. I don't get the chance to walk around islands that much.

TRUDY: (*Reluctantly*) Well . . .

DOUGLAS: Thank you for all your hospitality today. You've been very kind. You really have. (*He starts to move back towards the gate.*) Straight down the hill, I take it?

TRUDY: Yes. Only when you get to the fork that leads to the sea – the one we took – go right instead of left.

DOUGLAS: Simple enough. Well. See you tomorrow, Trudy.

TRUDY: Goodnight, Douglas.

DOUGLAS: (*Turning in the gateway*) Er . . . (*Smiling.*) There's one thing I wouldn't have minded, I suppose. Not that you could have given it to me. But since you mentioned wanting things . . .

TRUDY: What's that? Anything we –

DOUGLAS: No, I was just thinking. I was a hero, I suppose, for all of a year. People wrote to me. Sent for my photograph. Asked my advice. Listened to what I had to say. I think it would have been nice to have been a hero for a bit longer . . .

TRUDY: You still are –

DOUGLAS: . . . silly. I'd probably never have missed it, only . . .

TRUDY: – to people like Nerys you are. And I bet there are others who still remember . . .

DOUGLAS: No, I think I'm best remembered now as the idiot who tackled an armed robber and nearly got someone's head blown off in the process. I think you ended up with the hero, Trudy, not poor old Nerys. You stick with him. You stick with Vic. If you're looking for heroes. See you in the morning.

(DOUGLAS *goes out through the gate.* TRUDY *stares after him.*)

TRUDY: (*Faintly*) Yes . . .

(*She gets up to go into the house. Then decides that, if she's going to cry, she'd better cry out here. She sits down again in the shadows. She hugs herself and starts to weep quietly and privately.*

In a little while, there is a faint slapping sound from the direction

74

of the swimming pool. TRUDY *becomes aware of this and stops crying to listen.* SHARON *appears, walking along the side of the swimming pool towards the deep end. She has on her black wetsuit, rubber helmet and flippers. She carries a weighted diving belt. She is also crying. In fact, she is in a desperate, heart-broken state. She stops at the end of the swimming pool, a tragi-comic, fat, black, rubber-clad figure.*

TRUDY *watches her, astonished.* SHARON, *unaware she is being watched, looks towards the house and starts to fasten the diving belt about her waist.)*

(*Cautiously*) Sharon? Sharon . . . What are you doing there?

SHARON: (*Between sobs*) Mrs Parks . . .

TRUDY: What are you doing, Sharon?

SHARON: I'm going to kill myself, Mrs Parks.

TRUDY: (*Moving to her, alarmed*) You are going to what?

SHARON: I'm sorry, Mrs Parks. I love him so much, and he doesn't care about me at all.

TRUDY: Sharon . . .

SHARON: (*As in one breath*) He just says I'm fat and I've got to get thin and I've tried to get thin but I can't get thin whatever I do because when he says he doesn't love me I just keep eating because I'm so unhappy you see and then when I eat then I just get fatter you see and then he doesn't love me . . . and I love him so much, Mrs Parks, and I'm ever so sorry . . .

TRUDY: Yes . . . I'm sorry, Sharon . . . I know how it is, believe me I do . . .

SHARON: No, you don't – you can't . . .

TRUDY: Yes, I do. I promise, Sharon, I do . . .

SHARON: Nobody knows –

(*During the next, the music from the house stops as the record comes to an end.*)

TRUDY: Sharon, it's a passing thing, I promise. It's something we all go through. Most of us. God help us. It'll pass . . .

SHARON: No, it won't pass. I've loved Vic for years . . .

TRUDY: Years? What do you mean, years? You've only been with us two months . . .

SHARON: I seen him on the telly. I used to watch him on the

telly and I used to write to him on *Ask Vic* and he used to write back to me, he did, I promise . . .

TRUDY: Sharon, he gets thousands of letters a week. He doesn't even read them, let alone write back . . .

SHARON: He did, he wrote to me and it was in his writing. And he used to tell us on the telly if we had problems how to deal with them and not to worry and then when I got this job working for him I just thought it was going to be so wonderful and he's just been horrible to me . . . I don't know what I've done . . . What have I done wrong, Mrs Parks?

(*During the next*, VIC *comes out of the house and listens, unnoticed.*)

TRUDY: (*Fiercely*) The only thing you did wrong, Sharon . . . the one and only thing you ever did wrong was to love him in the first place . . . Because he is not a man to love, Sharon, I promise you. Not if you can possibly avoid it. I speak as one who has tried for eight years, Sharon, to keep loving him. While that bastard has abused me and ignored me and taken me for granted – while he has been screwing his way round Television Centre and half of ITV – I have looked after his kids and his house and his bloody, bad-tempered old mother in Beckenham . . . And I have tried to keep loving him . . . I swear to God I have tried. And if you are honestly clinging on to life in the hope of getting one tiny scrap of care or consideration back from that self-centred, selfish – scum bucket – then all I can say is, you'd better jump in there now, Sharon, and cut your losses.

(SHARON, *understandably, is a little bemused by this outburst. She stands indecisively.* VIC *steps out further on to the patio. Both women see him for the first time.*)

VIC: Well, well. You know what they say. You never hear good about yourself, do you?

TRUDY: Tell her, Vic. Talk to the girl, for God's sake.

VIC: Tell her what?

TRUDY: I just caught her trying to drown herself . . .

VIC: (*Amused*) What?

TRUDY: Vic, talk to her . . .

VIC: What do you want to drown yourself for, Sharon?

TRUDY: Why do you think . . . ?

VIC: I have no idea. I have no idea why this great big girl should want to drown herself . . .

(SHARON *sobs and finishes fastening her belt.*)

TRUDY: Vic . . .

VIC: Why? Just tell me?

TRUDY: Because of what you've said to her. Done to her.

VIC: What?

TRUDY: Whatever you said – whatever you did. I don't know. I don't want to know . . .

VIC: I've never laid a finger on her, have I? Sharon, tell her, I've never laid a finger on you . . . Have I? Eh?

SHARON: (*Unhappily*) No, Mr Parks . . .

VIC: There you are. No. She confirms that . . .

TRUDY: (*Shouting*) You know bloody well what you've done to her, Vic, now do something about it . . .

VIC: Right, that's it, forget it. I am not being shouted at. Let her jump . . .

(*He turns to move into the house.* SHARON *prepares to jump into the pool.*)

TRUDY: (*Yelling*) Vic . . .

VIC: (*Furiously*) Let the stupid cow drown herself, what do I care? Go on. Jump, jump, jump then . . .

(SHARON *jumps into the pool. Weighted down by her diver's belt, she sinks rapidly under the dark water and vanishes in a trail of bubbles.*)

TRUDY: (*Screaming*) SHARON!

VIC: (*Surprised* SHARON *has done it*) Bloody hell!

(VIC *moves towards the pool.*)

TRUDY: Vic, get her out. Dive in and get her out, for God's sake . . .

VIC: I'm not diving in there. Not in these clothes.

TRUDY: Vic, the girl is drowning.

VIC: She's not drowning. She can stay under for hours. She's built like a bathyscope . . .

TRUDY: Are you going in to get her, or not?

VIC: You dive in.

TRUDY: I can't get her out, she's far too big for me, she's enormous, Vic . . .

VIC: We could sprinkle rum babas on the surface, that'll bring her up . . .

TRUDY: You bastard . . . (*Desperately.*) Oh, dear God. (*Running to the gate and yelling.*) Douglas! Douglas! He's gone . . .

VIC: (*Peering into the pool, meanwhile*) Sharon! I can see you down there, Sharon.

TRUDY: (*Running to the house and calling.*) Kenny! Kenny, come out here, please!

VIC: Kenny went down to the shop – we were running out of vino . . .

TRUDY: If she dies, Vic. If that girl dies . . .

VIC: Nobody would miss her except the national union of bakers . . .

TRUDY: (*Running at him in fury*) You . . . God, I hate you! I really so hate you! (*She attacks him with both her fists.*)

VIC: (*Amused and fending her off easily*) Hey, hey, hey!

TRUDY: (*Beating at him*) I'd so love to . . . hurt you . . . like you . . . hurt . . . other people, sometimes . . .

(*She lands a blow that* VIC *doesn't care for. He takes her a little more seriously.*)

VIC: Oi! Now, Trudy! That's enough. You've had your fun . . .

(*He starts to pinion her arms to protect himself.* TRUDY *continues to fight and* VIC *is forced to turn her away from him and grab her neck in the crook of his arm in a traditional headhold whilst pinioning her arms with his other hand.* TRUDY *is finally incapacitated. She remains there, exhausted and infuriated by her impotence against his superior strength.*

Barely have they finished struggling when DOUGLAS *runs back into the garden through the gate. He is halfway to the house before he sees* VIC *and* TRUDY.)

DOUGLAS: (*As he enters*) What's the problem? I – (DOUGLAS *stops and stares at them in amazement.*)

TRUDY: (*Weakly, choking in* VIC's *grip*) Douglas . . . please!

VIC: (*Calmly*) Now, it's all right. Don't get excited and nobody'll get hurt, all right?

(DOUGLAS *reacts like a charger on hearing the bugle call. He*

gives a sudden wild yell of fury and rushes at VIC *head down.*)
DOUGLAS: Aaaaarrrrgggghhhh!
VIC: (*Startled*) Jesus!
(VIC *pushes* TRUDY *to one side in order to defend himself – not for the first time in his life – from Douglas's sudden wild onslaught.* DOUGLAS *catches* VIC *in the midriff.* TRUDY *screams.* VIC *grunts with pain, winded. Both men lose their balance.* VIC *topples into the pool.* DOUGLAS *is left kneeling on the edge, slightly winded himself.*)
TRUDY: Douglas? Are you all right?
DOUGLAS: Yes, I . . . I'm . . . I'm sorry, I . . . Where's Vic?
TRUDY: He's in the . . .
(*As she starts to speak,* VIC's *hand grips the edge of the pool. He hauls himself up. He looks very dangerous.*)
VIC: (*Breathless*) Right. There is about to be some serious damage done, I can tell you . . .(*Pointing at* DOUGLAS *and* TRUDY *in turn.*) To you. And to you. All right?
(DOUGLAS *and* TRUDY *draw back, nervously.* VIC *seems about to climb out of the pool.*
Suddenly the waters part and a large black shape, barely recognizable as SHARON, *breaks surface and seizes hold of* VIC *around the neck from behind.*)
As soon as I've . . . Uurrgghhh!
(*He is dragged under the water by* SHARON's *sheer weight.*)
DOUGLAS: (*Genuinely alarmed*) Oh, my goodness, what is it, a whale?
TRUDY: No, it's Sharon . . .
(*There is a great deal of frenzied threshing about under the water. Rather like an old Johnny Weissmuller film.* TRUDY *and* DOUGLAS *watch, unable to do much else.*)
TRUDY: (*During this, vainly*) Sharon . . . Vic . . .
DOUGLAS: (*Likewise*) Vic . . . Sharon . . .
(*The waters finally still.* SHARON *comes up for air and props herself against the side of the pool, breathlessly and strangely happy.* TRUDY *and* DOUGLAS *approach her cautiously.*)
TRUDY: Sharon . . . ?
DOUGLAS: Sharon . . . ?
TRUDY: Are you all right?

SHARON: (*Gathering enough breath to speak*) Yes, thank you, Mrs Parks . . .

DOUGLAS: (*Trying to calm her desperate breathing*) Easy. Easy now . . .

TRUDY: (*A sudden thought*) Sharon, where is Mr Parks?

SHARON: (*Apologetically*) I'm standing on him, Mrs Parks.
(TRUDY *and* DOUGLAS *react with alarm*.)

DOUGLAS: Sharon, for goodness sake . . .

TRUDY: (*With* DOUGLAS) For God's sake, get off him . . .
(*Together, they start to haul* SHARON *out of the water*.)

SHARON: (*As they do so*) I'm very sorry, Mrs Parks . . .

TRUDY: All right, Sharon, all right. Out you come now.
(*They land her on the poolside like a large, beached mammal.*
VIC *floats to the surface. Unconscious or worse.* SHARON *lies
panting while* TRUDY *and* DOUGLAS *pull* VIC *from the water*.)
(*To* DOUGLAS) Turn him over, we must get the water out of him . . .

DOUGLAS: Right.
(*They turn* VIC *over*.)

SHARON: (*As they do so*) Can I give him the kiss of life, Mrs Parks . . . ?

TRUDY: No, you can't, Sharon. Stay there, please.
(*She and* DOUGLAS *try to work on* VIC *rather ineffectually*.)
I don't know what you do. I think you have to pump his ribs somehow . . .

DOUGLAS: I'm afraid I don't really have much of an idea . . . Me and water, you know . . .

SHARON: (*Heaving herself up*) Here, let me . . .

TRUDY: No, Sharon, I'd rather you . . .

SHARON: It's all right, Mrs Parks, I've got my life-saver's medal.

TRUDY: (*Rather surprised*) You have?

SHARON: In the Huddersfield baths. Here, let me . . .
(SHARON *takes over from* TRUDY *and* DOUGLAS. *She sits
astride* VIC *and pumps away vigorously.* TRUDY *and* DOUGLAS
watch her anxiously.)

TRUDY: Anything . . . ?

SHARON: No, I don't think he's . . . He's not responding.

TRUDY: Oh, God.

SHARON: Hang on.

(*She rolls* VIC *over and tries the kiss of life a couple of times. There is no response.*)

TRUDY: (*Anxiously*) No?

SHARON: No. I'm sorry, Mrs Parks, I . . . (*Starting to cry as the realization finally hits her.*) I'm sorry. I'm ever so sorry . . . (*She kneels weeping again. A silence.*)

TRUDY: I don't know what we're going to do. I don't know. (*Silence.*)

What are we going to do?

DOUGLAS: I suppose we'll have to report it. To the police, won't we?

TRUDY: If we report it, we'll have to tell them everything. We'll have to tell them it was Sharon. We can't have Sharon blamed for this . . .

SHARON: (*Tearfully*) I didn't mean to, Mrs Parks . . .

TRUDY: (*Comforting her*) It's all right, Sharon, it's all right. (*She considers.*) OK, I'll tell you what we're going to do. We're all going to have to tell the same story, all right? Douglas?

DOUGLAS: Yes?

TRUDY: Sharon? Are you listening to me?

SHARON: Yes, Mrs Parks.

TRUDY: We're going to have to say this. Vic was very drunk – that's true, anyway – and he came out here on his own and must have decided to take a swim. And, Sharon, you were upstairs and you heard the splash and you rushed downstairs and called for help – only Kenny wasn't in –

DOUGLAS: What about the couple? You know, the Spanish couple? Do they live in?

TRUDY: Yes, but they'll be watching television, they'd never have heard . . . And then you came out here, Sharon, you see . . . ?

SHARON: Yes . . .

TRUDY: And you found Mr Parks floating unconscious in the water –

DOUGLAS: In all his clothes?

TRUDY: Yes. Good point. We'd better take some of those off him . . .

SHARON: (*Starting at once*) Right . . .

TRUDY: No, let me finish. And then you dived in, Sharon –

SHARON: Was I wearing my wetsuit?

TRUDY: No. Well done. You'd better take that off, too.

SHARON: What, now?

TRUDY: Yes.

SHARON: (*Softly*) I've got nothing underneath, Mrs Parks.

TRUDY: (*Angrily*) Sharon, we are talking about murder. If you are going to worry about being done for indecent exposure . . .

SHARON: (*Starting*) Yes, Mrs Parks . . . (*She begins to unfasten her belt.*)

TRUDY: No, let me finish first. And then, finally, Douglas and I came back from our walk in time to find you trying to revive Vic. But to no avail. How does that sound?

SHARON: Brilliant.

TRUDY: (*To* DOUGLAS) All right?

DOUGLAS: (*Obviously unhappy*) Yes. I don't see an alternative, really, but –

TRUDY: (*Taking this as agreement*) Sharon, strip off. Douglas, help me with Vic . . . Quick as you can, everyone.

(*The three work in silence, concentrating on their tasks.* SHARON *takes off her belt, then her hood and flippers.* DOUGLAS *and* TRUDY *start to undress* VIC *with difficulty, removing his jacket, shirt, shoes and socks. As they are doing this, they are unaware of the audience that starts to assemble. Through the back gate,* KENNY *enters. He has the jeep keys, having just returned from the shops. He carries a couple of loose bottles of wine. Behind him comes* RUY, *who carries the bulk of their purchase, namely a full case of wine. They stop and watch the proceedings with horrified fascination. Soon after,* MARTA *comes out from the house with a tray, looking for stray dirty glasses. She stops, likewise, to watch suspiciously.* SHARON *is about to do the final lap of her striptease and remove her wetsuit. She is on the point of doing this when she becomes aware of their audience. She freezes, open-mouthed, staring.* TRUDY *and* DOUGLAS *take a second or so longer to realize. They are on the point of removing* VIC's *trousers.*)

(*To* DOUGLAS) Right. You pull off his trousers, while I hold him . . .

82

DOUGLAS: (*Struggling*) Yes.
    (*It is a difficult operation.*)
TRUDY: God, he's a weight . . . Sharon, can you help us?
    (*They struggle again.*)
DOUGLAS: Hang on.
TRUDY: He's so . . . He's so . . . Sharon, don't just stand there –
    please – come and . . .
    (TRUDY *finally becomes aware of why* SHARON *has frozen.*
    DOUGLAS *is the last to notice. They stand up, guiltily.*)
KENNY: What the hell is going on?
    (*Silence.* VIC, *released, flops over, very obviously dead.*)
    What have you done to him? What have you done to Vic?
TRUDY: (*Feebly*) We were just . . . We were just . . . undressing
    him.
KENNY: What's happened? He looks dead. Is he dead?
TRUDY: (*Softly*) Yes, he's dead.
MARTA: (*Crossing herself, whispering*) Mr Vic!
RUY: (*Likewise, crossing the carton of wine*) Mr Vic!
KENNY: (*Softly*) Jesus . . . I think I'm going to have to phone the
    police, aren't I?
DOUGLAS: Yes, I think you are . . .
    (SHARON *whimpers.*)
TRUDY: No!
KENNY: How did it happen, Trudy? I need to know.
TRUDY: Well . . .
SHARON: Well . . .
DOUGLAS: (*Stepping forward unexpectedly*) It's all right, leave it to
    me. (*To* TRUDY *and* SHARON.) I'm sorry. There's no other
    way. There's only one thing worth telling and that's the
    truth.
KENNY: Quite right. It's my experience, in cases like this, that
    there's absolutely nothing like the truth. Absolutely –
    nothing like it at all.
    (*Before* DOUGLAS *can start to explain,* ASHLEY BARNES, *a TV
    floor manager complete with two-way radio, steps on to the floor,
    appearing unexpectedly and as from nowhere. The lights close
    down to a small area round him, momentarily.*)
ASHLEY: (*With great authority*) Sorry, everyone. We need to stop

for just a second. Sorry. Bear with us, we won't be two seconds. (*Listening to instructions from his earpiece.*) Mmm . . . yes . . . mmm . . . hmm-mmm . . . yes . . . OK . . . I see . . . yes . . .

(*While* ASHLEY *listens, the general lighting returns. The actors playing* VIC, DOUGLAS, TRUDY, SHARON, KENNY, RUY *and* MARTA *have left the stage to be replaced by their counterpart 'TV' actors, who are to be used to mime out scripted events. This switch should have occurred as swiftly and unobtrusively as possible. Although none of the replacement performers concerned are particularly miscast (it is sufficient that they are different), there have been one or two cosmetic improvements. The new* SHARON *is slim and really quite attractive in her shapely wetsuit. She has shed the helmet and has her hair tied back.* VIC *is possibly glamorized a little, too, in an anti-hero sort of way. He's certainly less drunk.* RUY *and* MARTA *are a shade more 'Spanish'. All the clothing – apart from Sharon's – is similar but not identical to their original counterparts. The ensuing action is as silent as possible, leaving* JILL's *voice to serve as a 'voice-over' to it.*)

(*Having received final instructions*) OK. I'm afraid we have to go back just to Sharon jumping in the pool.

(*The actors immediately start to move.*)

My apologies, everyone, this is purely for cameras. Many apologies. We'll go when you're ready, everyone . . . (*To the audience.*) Do bear with us once again, ladies and gentlemen. I'm afraid these things do happen. I crave your patience.

(*The replacement* VIC *goes off into the house, gathering up his wet clothes as he goes. Replacement* MARTA *precedes him. Replacement* SHARON *goes off along the pool taking her discarded gear with her. The other replacements go off,* TRUDY *and* DOUGLAS *following* RUY *and* KENNY *out through the gate. As this happens, the real* JILL *comes on from the house. She is in her smart presenter's outfit. She stands on the patio, waiting. She carries a clipboard. She is in her most tense, unsmiling, professional mood at present.*)

Sorry, Jill. We'll need to go from the top of that final sequence again.

JILL: The final sequence?
ASHLEY: From where she jumps in.
JILL: OK.

> (*She consults her clipboard. The lighting changes slightly.*
> *Although the general area stays lit, there is a bright 'special' on*
> JILL.)

ASHLEY: (*Listening to a final instruction from his earpiece*) OK?
Thank you, Jill. (*Yelling.*) Quiet studio, please. (*To* JILL.) In
your own time, Jill, whenever you're ready.

> (*He moves back as he speaks. As* ASHLEY *goes off,* JILL
> *hesitates a second, then moves up a couple of gears in order to do*
> *her piece to camera.*)

JILL: And so to the final events of that tragic night. The crew and
I had finished for the day and had gone back to our hotel to
have dinner. For a description of what followed we must
rely, therefore, on the testimonies of first Sharon, the nanny,
then Douglas and Trudy, and finally Vic's manager,
Kenneth Collins. Piecing together these various eyewitness
accounts, the following is almost certainly a true picture of
what occurred.

> (*As* JILL *speaks, the previous scene is enacted again. If the facts*
> *are different, then so are the performers.*)

Trudy, in the company of Douglas Beechey, had decided to
take a stroll to the beach. Kenneth Collins had walked with
Ruy, the gardener, to the local store to buy extra provisions.
And whilst Marta, the maid, was preparing supper in the
kitchen, Vic sat in the living room relaxing and listening to
some of his favourite country and western music.

> (*She pauses for a second to allow the strains of pre-recorded*
> *background country and western music to filter from the direction*
> *of the house. This is not the same as previously heard, probably*
> *more romantic. It plays gently under the rest of Jill's speech,*
> *accompanying the action that follows. The replacement* SHARON
> *enters during the next and stands gazing into the pool and slowly*
> *fastening on her diving belt.*)

Unknown to any of them, it was at this stage that the
children's nanny, Sharon Giffin, decided that her life was no
longer worth living. She resolved to kill herself. Perhaps the

eventual realization that her secret, undeclared passion for
Vic Parks could never be reciprocated, combined with a
totally naïve misinterpretation of the kindness he had shown
to her whilst she worked there, proved too much for this
simple, semi-literate girl from Macclesfield. It was her good
fortune, even as she fastened on her weighted scuba diver's
belt and prepared to jump, that Vic happened to catch sight
of her through the open windows. Realizing at once her
intention, he rushed out to try and stop her –

(*The replacement* VIC *runs out of the house and stops for a minute
staring at* SHARON.)

But he was too late to stop her jumping –

(VIC *yells silently at* SHARON, *who jumps into the pool.* VIC
*starts to run to the pool, shedding his shirt and trousers as he does
so. He leaps into the pool after her.*)

What happened next is unclear. Trudy and Douglas arrived
back from their walk in time to see two figures struggling in
the water in the darkness.

(*Replacement* DOUGLAS *and replacement* TRUDY *have entered
and hurried at once to the swimming pool, where they haul*
SHARON *from the water, during the next, and bring her round.*)

Sharon, herself, has only the dimmest memory of being
hauled from the water in a semi-conscious state. At first,
both rescuers concentrated on reviving her, assuming that
Vic himself – a strong swimmer and in good physical
condition – had no need of assistance. By the time they
realized all was not well, it was already too late. In his violent
struggle with the desperate, frenzied girl, Vic Parks had
received a glancing blow, sufficient to knock him
unconscious and allow his lungs to fill with water.

(*Replacements* TRUDY *and* DOUGLAS, *under the last, re-enact
the sudden realization that* VIC *is still in the water. They locate
his body and start to pull him from the pool. As they do so,
replacements* KENNY *and* RUY *appear in the gateway.* RUY
carries a box of groceries. Replacement MARTA *appears in the
house doorway. She is wiping her hands on a kitchen towel and
has evidently been preparing food.*)

Despite frantic and repeated efforts, they were too late to

save him. When the others returned to the villa, they found themselves little more than powerless spectators, forced to witness the final act of a needless tragedy. That night marked not only the end of a life but the end of a living legend.

(*During this,* SHARON *sits exhausted,* TRUDY *and* DOUGLAS *make efforts to save* VIC. MARTA, KENNY *and* RUY *stand watching anxiously. Finally,* DOUGLAS *looks up from* VIC'*s body and shakes his head.* MARTA, KENNY *and* RUY *move in slowly and incredulously. They kneel with the others around the body, forming a moving and well-grouped tableau which then freezes while* JILL *concludes her speech.*)

How best to sum up Vic Parks? A man whose life, ironically, ended as violently as it had started. But in between how to describe him? Hero or villain? Latter-day saint or merely late-twentieth-century showman? The arguments will continue. Perhaps his best epitaph is a piece of advice given spontaneously to a young viewer to whom he said: 'Don't complain to me that people kick you when you're down. It's your own fault for lying there, isn't it?'

(*She sits in the chair in which she started the play. The music fades out or finishes gently. The lights, from now on, close down on* JILL. *The others remain frozen and are all but lost in the gloom. By the end of the next,* ASHLEY *has reappeared at the edge of the set. Jill's manner now lightens from the solemn/ reverent to the fireside/jokey level for her final wind up.*)

Sad to say, that's the last of *Their Paths Crossed*. If you enjoyed this short series but think that four wasn't *quite* enough, tell you what – why not drop them a line up there and let them know? Them. You know the ones I mean. As for me, I'm off to pastures new but I hope we'll meet again soon. Next week at this time – and quite coincidentally – the start of *The Very Best of Vic* – a series of twelve special programmes featuring selected highlights from his recent series. And don't forget, too, you Vic Parks devotees who happen to be in the London area next month, I'll be co-presenting what's planned to be the first of the Annual Midland Bank Vic Parks Awards for Youth – founded, of course, in memory of the man himself. That's at the Royal

Albert Hall on Saturday the 18th. There's still a few seats left. So do try to get along if you can. Remember, it's all in a very good cause. Oh, and incidentally, there's a fabulous country and western line up, too. But in the meantime, that's all from me, Jill Rillington. Bye for now. And mind how you go, won't you? Bye.

(JILL *smiles into the camera and holds her expression for a second or so.* ASHLEY *steps forward into the middle.*)

ASHLEY: Thank you, everyone. Just hold it a minute, please. We're waiting for clearance.

(*He waits. Patiently listening to his earpiece.*)

JILL: (*Sweetly, to the audience*) They just have to check that last bit through. See if we've managed to get it right this time. Won't be a second.

(*A pause. We wait. The actor playing replacement* VIC *is now sitting up and whistling quietly to himself. The others wait patiently.*)

ACTOR: (*the actor playing replacement* RUY) Jill . . . Jill!

JILL: Hallo?

ACTOR: I don't know if you noticed, but the second time I came on a tidge later at the end there. I hope that was OK.

JILL: (*Rather impatiently, the man is obviously a pain*) I'm sure that was fine, David . . .

ACTOR: I mean, I could do it again if they want it . . .

JILL: It was fine. I don't think they were on you, then, anyway.

ACTOR: (*Faintly disappointed*) Oh, right. Fair enough.

(ASHLEY *is getting instructions through his earpiece.*)

ASHLEY: (*Speaking to the gallery*) Yep . . . yeah . . . yep . . . Great, grand, thank you. Thank you, Jill, thank you very much, everyone. They're very happy with that. Thank you.

(*The* ACTORS *leave by the various exits.*)

JILL: (*As she goes, cheerily to the audience*) Bye.

ASHLEY: (*Briskly and brightly, it is a well-oiled routine*) Right. Ladies and gentlemen, just before you leave – I know you're all dying to get home. One last little request – I know, I've been making requests all evening, but this, I promise you, is my last request for just one vast burst of your really *warmest* applause. That I know only you can give me. We have yet,

you see, to record one little further item. Which is, of course, our final credits sequence. That's when all those names of people you've never even *heard* of, doing jobs you don't even know what they *are*, this is when their names go *racing* across your screen while you're busy putting the cat out and couldn't care less anyway. Well, fair enough, but they've got to be there and, more important, one of the names is mine, so when you see that go through – my name is Ashley Barnes, by the way – watch out for it – Ashley Barnes – special loud applause for that, then I get more money, right . . . Seriously, as much *warm* applause as you can give us. Let's tell the people at home what a really good time you've had and then who knows, perhaps they'll believe they've had a good one, too. And we'll get a second series after all. All right? So on my signal – we'll be going with the final music . . . In just a few seconds. (*Slight pause.*) I hope. (*Pause.*) Yes, here we go. (ASHLEY *stands. He smiles at the audience. He gets the countdown from the gallery. He holds up his hand and counts down with his fingers, mouthing silently with this.*) Five . . . four . . . three . . . two . . .
(*He starts the applause. The final credit music plays under this. The curtain call is taken. The actors leave the stage. The music stops.*)
Thank you all very much indeed. Goodnight. Get home safely now. (*As he moves away from the floor.*) Thank you very much, studio.
(*The stage lights snap off to be replaced with the house lights.*)